The Plains of Promise

by

KERRY ALLYNE

Harlequin Books

TORONTO • LONDON • NEW YORK • AMSTERDAM
SYDNEY • HAMBURG • PARIS

Original hardcover edition published in 1979
by Mills & Boon Limited

ISBN 0-373-02283-2

Harlequin edition published September 1979

Copyright © 1979 by Kerry Allyne
Philippine copyright 1979. Australian copyright 1979.

All rights reserved. Except for use in any review, the reproduction or utilization of
this work in whole or in part in any form by any electronic, mechanical or other
means, now known or hereafter invented, including xerography, photocopying
and recording, or in any information storage or retrieval system, is forbidden
without the permission of the publisher. All the characters in this book have no
existence outside the imagination of the author and have no relation whatsoever
to anyone bearing the same name or names. They are not even distantly
inspired by any individual known or unknown to the author, and all the incidents
are pure invention.

The Harlequin trademark, consisting of the word HARLEQUIN and the portrayal
of a Harlequin, is registered in the United States Patent Office and in the Canada
Trade Marks Office.

Printed in U.S.A.

CHAPTER ONE

At first it was almost impossible to distinguish anything through the dancing heat haze which wavered over the landscape, but the other three occupants of the car were only too willing to take Brad Keogh's word for it when, after having been on the road continuously since the dark hours of the night before, he finally exclaimed, 'There's Fairfax Downs homestead now!'

Struggling upwards from her reclining position on the seat beside him, Gwayne adjusted her dark glasses more firmly on her slim, tip-tilted nose and ran combing fingers through the rumpled curls of her long bright auburn hair. A nod of her head included the couple in the back seat.

'We were beginning to think the place was only a figment of your imagination,' she teased, peering interestedly through the windscreen into the distance. 'It seemed as if we were never going to arrive.'

'I'm sure that's because this heat makes every mile seem like ten,' interposed Donna from behind them as she too squinted into the glaring sunlight which was bathing the wildflower-strewn plains. 'No wonder it always looks so still out here—nothing's got the energy to move!'

Next to her Warren was the last to throw off the somnolent lethargy which had been enveloping all of them for the latter part of their nine-hundred-mile journey north-west from Sydney and now remarked, 'It's a lot greener than I expected, though. Have they had rain recently, Brad?'

The wiry shoulders in front of him shrugged impassively. 'Looks as if they could have done. I can't remember it ever having had this much ground cover before.'

'You used to come here quite often, then?' Gwayne took her eyes from the flamboyant scenery to ask.

He nodded shortly. 'The whole family did up until the time my Aunt Karen and her husband were killed in a light plane crash some twelve years ago, but only rarely since then.'

'In that case you must be looking forward to seeing your cousin again after so long,' she surmised with a smile.

'Must I?'

Under cover of her sunglasses Gwayne's brows arched expressively. Considering it had been Brad's suggestion that the four of them should spend their holidays together on Fairfax Downs, his somewhat sardonic counter-question came as something of a surprise. From the time he had first mentioned the idea she had automatically assumed that he and his cousin enjoyed a friendly relationship, but now she found herself wondering if perhaps she should have reserved judgment on that score.

'Oh, look! You can see the homestead properly now.'

With Donna's pleased announcement, Gwayne's curious thoughts were quickly dispersed and her own gaze came up to search out the building from amongst a profusion of brilliantly flowering shrubs and delicately fronded shade trees as they drew closer. It was Warren's long-drawn-out whistle of appreciation from between his teeth which initially gave voice to their thoughts, however, for not only did the homestead seem to cover an enormous area of ground, but it was picturesquely comprised of a series of identical gabled pavilions connected to one another by cooling breeze-ways; the whole structure encompassed by a wide polished verandah adorned with potted plants, a strategically placed wrought iron lace table and chairs, and a variety of colourful loungers.

As the car swept along the red-gravelled driveway a sprinkler began to shower the closely cropped emerald green lawn with droplets of water which shone like jewels in the lowering rays of the afternoon sun, and a flock of galahs wheeled overhead, showing themselves first silver-grey and then rose-pink against the azure blue vault of the sky.

'Good heavens, Brad, fancy you having a cousin who owns a place like this,' Donna grinned as she gratefully swung her long legs out of the vehicle and stood looking at the imposing residence. 'It sure leaves our three-bedroomed brick veneers in town for dead, doesn't it?'

'You can say that again,' Warren endorsed her comments with feeling, his keen brown gaze missing nothing as he sauntered around to the boot of the car and began extracting their luggage. 'It appears you were born into the wrong branch of the family, eh, mate?' he laughed across at his boyhood friend.

An anticipatory smile curved Gwayne's mobile mouth as she waited for one of Brad's normally light-hearted quips to be given in response to their raillery, but it never came. Instead, Brad's lips thinned angrily as a heavy scowl descended on to his face and he snapped back irritably,

'You can leave those! There's staff here who are paid to carry the luggage inside.'

It was hard for Gwayne to keep the astonishment she

was feeling from showing in her expression, but Warren had no such reservations.

'Hell, man, what's got into you?' he frowned. 'I figured it was good enough of your cousin to let us all stay here. I wasn't expecting to be waited on hand and foot as well.'

Suddenly Brad grinned, relieving all their anxieties. 'Don't worry, you won't be,' he retorted in his more natural manner. 'I was planning on asking if we could set ourselves up in the shearers' quarters instead of the homestead. That way we can please ourselves when we eat and at what times we come and go.'

'You mean, do all our own cooking, etcetera?' queried Donna.

'That's right. There's stoves and showers and anything else we might need down there, and it would keep us out of *their* hair.' A sharp inclination of his head indicated the house.

Gwayne and Donna exchanged shrugs. 'Sounds okay to us,' they both agreed.

'Then I may as well leave the luggage where it is,' Warren half laughed. 'There's no sense in taking it out if we're not staying in the homestead.'

The next moment a tall white-haired woman in her late fifties hurried out on to the verandah, her clear blue eyes evincing a welcome, her dress of pink silk portraying a simple but expensive elegance.

'Ah, Brad, you've arrived at last,' she smiled warmly as she approached them. 'I'm sorry I wasn't able to greet you as soon as the car drew up, but I was just taking down a message from Arleen Halford. She wanted to know if Regan was back yet.'

Brad's mouth turned down at the corners in unconcealed dislike. 'I thought she was married and had left the area years ago,' he stated tersely.

'Oh, she was, dear, but she's divorced now and living with her parents again,' he was informed matter-of-factly. 'You know how it is these days, married one year, separated the next, and then divorced. No one seems to take their marriage vows seriously any more. That is, if they bother to make them at all.'

'Yes, well, I can't say I'm surprised in Arleen's case. I could never imagine her as a loving wife,' he snorted disparagingly, and then, remembering, 'But I apologise, I haven't introduced you yet. Gwayne Peters, Donna Benson, and Warren Harris,' he indicated each of them in turn, 'my aunt by marriage, Charlotte Fairfax.'

'I'm very pleased to meet you all,' the older woman returned their separate deferences kindly and began ushering them towards the steps. 'Any friends of Brad's are most welcome, and as I'm sure you could all do with one after your long journey, why don't we have a nice cool drink on the verandah and maybe get to know each other a little better, hmm?'

This suggestion was hailed with great enthusiasm by the four travellers and it was only a matter of minutes before they were duly seated around the table they had espied earlier and were partaking of their chosen form of refreshment as Charlotte Fairfax eyed her nephew enquiringly.

'When your mother rang me about your intended visit she said she didn't know how long you would be staying with us. I do hope it's for longer than the last time you came, though, Brad. We see you so rarely that a week just isn't enough time to catch up on everything that's been happening,' she protested.

'Well, there should be enough time this year,' he smiled in return. 'We were planning to stay for the whole four weeks. If that's all right with you, of course?'

'As if you need to ask!' came the prompt but obviously pleased remonstrance. 'Stay as long as you like. You know I love having visitors.'

'That's very kind of you, Miss Fairfax,' Gwayne now spoke for the first time since moving on to the verandah, and trusted that she was correct in her form of address because she couldn't see any other rings, apart from a pearl dress ring on that woman's fingers, to indicate she was married. 'It's not everyone who would welcome three strangers into their home so willingly.'

'Think nothing of it, my dear,' Charlotte waved aside her gratitude easily. 'It's not as if we don't have the room.'

Brad cleared his throat and moved forward on his chair. 'Well, actually in that regard, Aunt Charlotte, we were wondering if we couldn't manage for ourselves in the shearers' quarters. It would save any disruptions to the homestead and—and we wouldn't disturb anyone if we wanted to leave early in the mornings or—or return late at night,' he explained a trifle uncomfortably.

His aunt looked at him in some astonishment. 'Goodness, I don't think it would be possible for you to leave any earlier in the mornings than Regan does, and he's not often home again before dark,' she relayed with a smile. 'Besides, the shearers themselves will be moving in next week.'

'That's early for them, isn't it?' Brad sounded decidedly put out by the information. 'I thought there was another couple of months to go before they arrived.'

'There used to be,' Charlotte concurred amiably, 'but Regan moved our shearing time forward a few seasons ago, for greater fly control amongst other things, and he's been more than satisfied with the results from the change ever since.'

'Then that settles that!'

Never had Gwayne heard Brad sound so disgruntled in all the five months she had known him, and she stared across at him with a perplexed frown furrowing her forehead. If, as it was unfortunately beginning to seem, he wasn't happy about being here, then why on earth had he suggested they come? So far his attitude didn't augur well for an enjoyable holiday for any of them!

'And now, why don't you tell me something about yourselves?' Charlotte's eyes ranged over them interestedly. 'How did you all come to meet?'

'Well, let's see ... it had better be an abridged version or else we're likely to be sitting here for a very long time,' Warren responded with a laugh, then he proceeded to explain, 'I've known Brad ever since we were in primary school together. Donna and Gwayne work for the same firm of engineers, became friends, and now share a flat together. I met Donna last summer while surfboard riding at the beach—we collided on the same wave, actually ...'

'When his board sliced mine clean in two,' put in Donna with a mock grimace.

'And we've been meeting ever since,' he continued. 'A few months ago we decided to try a little matchmaking, introduced Gwayne to Brad, and lo and behold, our twosome has developed into a foursome.'

'It was fortunate you could all have your holidays at the same time.'

Sweeping her long dark hair away from her forehead, Donna took up the tale. 'Yes, well, I must admit that certainly took some arranging. In fact, I only managed to get away because one of the other girls in the office who was supposed to be having hers at this time cancelled them at the last minute owing to a mix-up in her bookings.'

Charlotte Fairfax smiled in response, but her gaze was clearly attracted to the redheaded girl seated beside her. As it had been on a number of occasions since they arrived, Gwayne noted.

'I do hope you don't mind my drawing attention to it, but your hair is a really beautiful and quite unusual colour, my dear,' she complimented before continuing on a warmly sympathetic note, 'although I suppose you would have a lot of trouble with sunburn if you're not careful.'

Gwayne's head nodded vigorously. 'Yes, very much so, I'm afraid.' The laugh which followed was a rueful one full of painful memories. 'It's been the bane of my life! Everyone else can shed as many articles of clothing as possible when they go to the beach. I usually end up having to do the exact opposite!'

'What she refuses to realise, of course, is that the rest of us would willingly trade our darker skins in exchange for just some of that extraordinarily eye-catching colouring of hers,' Donna broke in, looking down at her own smoothly bronzed arms with wry dissatisfaction. 'After all, what's so startling about a suntan in this country? Everyone's got one!'

'Except me!' Gwayne registered her protest on a plaintive note which set them all laughing.

A short while later Brad's aunt had them shown to their separate rooms so that they might have time to settle in and shower before dinner, and after Stan Wallace, the housekeeper's chubby husband and general handyman about the station, had deposited her cases in the room of the pavilion she was to share with her friend, Gwayne stood just inside the doorway and took stock of her surroundings.

It was a delightfully cool room with french doors leading on to the main verandah as well as the breeze-way, and even to her inexperienced gaze it was obvious that the intricately fashioned and richly upholstered furniture hadn't been mass-produced, while the highly polished cedar flooring and wall panelling gave off a deep red gleam the like of which she had only heard about but never seen before.

There was an indefinable feeling of permanence and solidity about Fairfax Downs which appealed strongly to some unfulfilled force inside her, and not only because it was the first time in the whole of her twenty-one years that she had had a bedroom all to herself. Left proverbially on the doorstep of the Ramsay Home for Children when she was only a few months old, she had shared a dormitory with many others until she had started work and begun sharing their one-bedroomed flat with Donna. Now an unbelievable sense of unbounded space assailed her and, on a sudden impulse to capture it in full, she pirouetted dreamily across the room towards the silk-covered bed with her arms stretched wide.

'I can leave again if I'm interrupting anything important.'

The sound of Donna's highly amused voice coming from the doorway of the bathroom which connected the two rooms had Gwayne dropping on to the side of the bed abruptly, a wide grin curving her mouth.

'Don't mind me, I was only taking some positive enjoyment from having a room all to myself for the very first time,' she twinkled. 'What's your room like?'

'Much of a muchness. The furniture's different but the quality's the same.' Donna's dark brown eyes rolled implicitly. 'God, they must be loaded!'

'That thought had occurred to me too,' dryly.

'Have you ever seen so much cedar and teak in all your life?' the other girl went on as she pointed to the floor and walls as well as the exposed ceiling beams. 'Why, the house itself would have to be worth a fortune just in the timber alone, without taking in any of the contents!'

It was a far cry from their small cramped flat and even farther from the utilitarian orphanage where Gwayne had grown up, and her expression sobered rapidly.

'Mmm, it makes you feel a little out of place somehow, doesn't it?'

'If by that you mean that it makes me feel somewhat humdrum, you could be right,' Donna acknowledged. 'But if you mean that I'll be feeling too out of my depth to enjoy myself while I'm here, not a chance! This is the opportunity of a lifetime and I don't intend to miss out on it. Just think of the social circles these people move in, my love, and let that be your guide. Who knows who we might be lucky enough to meet while we're here?' she concluded with a shrewdly expectant smile.

Gwayne's warm sherry-coloured eyes widened as she heard her friend out and Donna's designs became clear. 'But I thought you were keen on Warren! That sort of attitude is hardly fair to him, is it?' she demurred.

'Oh, come on, Gwayne, don't be so naïve! Having spent almost the whole of your life so far in an orphanage, I would have thought you'd be the biggest realist of any of us,' Donna retorted with fond exasperation. 'Of course I'm keen on Warren—I wouldn't have gone out with him so often if I wasn't—but I'm not so enamoured of him that I'm blind to reality, or the fact that his job as a clerk isn't likely to lift us into the lap of luxury should we ever decide to marry. It's just as easy to fall for a rich man as a poor one. No, I'll correct that,' she amended with an incorrigible grin. 'I reckon it would be *easier* to fall for a rich one.'

'You don't think the man himself needs to be taken into consideration too?'

'Oh, naturally,' came the blithe return. 'He would have to be slim, trim, between twenty and forty, attractive, generous, kind, thoughtful, idolise *me* of course, and ...' She dissolved into a fit of laughter. 'Have I left anything out?'

'Apart from your original requirement of stacks of money, I don't think so,' Gwayne laughed with her. 'More to the point, though, do you think you've got a chance of meeting anyone with those qualifications during our four-week stay?'

'That all depends on how much entertaining they do, I guess,' Donna conceded consideringly. 'But from what I've heard they seem to socialise far more out here than people do in town these days, and with all those beaut little planes they all seem to own whizzing around the countryside you never know who's likely to drop in. While there's life there's hope.'

Gwayne rose to her feet and gave her friend a wry smile. 'Well, while you're dreaming about it I think I'll start unpacking and have a shower. I wouldn't like to keep them waiting for dinner on our first night here.'

'Mmm, you've got something there. It wouldn't create a very good impression, would it?' Donna began heading towards her own room again, saying over her shoulder as she went, 'If you're going to unpack I'll have my shower now. That way we won't both be wanting the bathroom at the same time.'

It didn't take long for Gwayne to put her few clothes away, or to make use of the cinnamon and cream tiled bathroom once Donna had vacated it, and then change into a slim-fitting dress of pale lilac silk jersey with a geometric pattern in dark mauve around the flaring hemline. As her creamy matt skin needed little embellishment she only applied a faint trace of a frosted coffee shadow to her eyelids and thickened her already dark lashes with mascara before adding a covering of light bronze to her softly curving lips. With her hair neatly disciplined by the judicious use of brush and comb she was preparing to see how Donna was progressing when a knock on the glass of the doors which opened to the breezeway announced Brad's arrival.

'My, aren't you a sight for sore eyes!' he smiled as he stepped over the threshold, his glance running over her shapely form appreciatively. 'You look absolutely stunning!'

'Why, thank you, kind sir,' Gwayne grinned, and sketched him a mock curtsey. 'Although I do wish you'd been a little more explicit regarding the style of homestead you were bringing us to. By the look of it, I would say the one long dress and one long skirt each which Donna and I brought won't nearly be enough.'

Brad shrugged indifferently, the edges of his mouth imperceptibly tightening. 'Don't let that worry you, I'm sure my dear cousin will find you quite attractive as it is without an extensive wardrobe to your credit.'

'Will he?' Gwayne slanted him a cool look from beneath curling lashes. 'Well, that wasn't my intention, or my reason for mentioning the matter, I can assure you! And especially since I've never met the man.'

He had the grace to look abashed as he sighed and caught at one of her hands to grip it tightly. 'I know, honey, I know! You're not the type and I'm a senseless idiot for implying that you might be,' he exclaimed contritely, releasing her fingers as suddenly as he had grasped them in order to thrust his hands into the pockets of his pants as he turned away to stare out through the doorway to the dusk-clouded gardens. 'It's always the damned same! I knew we should never have come here,' he muttered angrily beneath his breath.

'But you were the one who suggested it!' Gwayne couldn't help reminding him incredulously.

'Only I hadn't intended it to be taken seriously,' he divulged, scowling. 'But once Warren mentioned it to my mother that was the end of it. All I had drummed into me from then on was how it was expected of me to stay with my cousin if we were coming out this way. "After all, Regan never fails to call on us whenever he's in Sydney",' he repeated his parent's censure bitterly. 'In the end I gave in just for the sake of peace and quiet.'

'Oh, Brad,' she murmured helplessly, not knowing quite what to suggest. 'Is he really that difficult to get on with?'

'That's one way of putting it. He's a patronising so-and-so at the best of times.'

'In that case, I think it's better we don't stay, even if it means missing out on our holidays altogether.'

'What?' He swung back to face her indignantly. 'And give him a good laugh because he managed to make it too uncomfortable for us? Not on your life!'

'Then what are we going to do?' Gwayne demanded with some asperity, wishing he would make up his mind.

'Exactly what we planned, of course!' Brad informed her brusquely. 'We'll make full use of the conveniences and facilities available, and ignore him as much as possible in the process.'

'Won't that be a little hard to do, seeing he's our

host?' Her brows rose with delicate irony.

'Not if we put our minds to it, but if you and Donna are planning on giving him coy glances from inviting eyes like the rest of his female acquaintances do, then in all probability I expect my strategy will fail!' he retorted peevishly.

'And if you come up with any more remarks like that one then I'll be hoping it does! How dare you make such a rotten suggestion, Brad?' she flared, stung by his unfounded insinuation. 'If you don't like it here then let's leave . . . and to hell with what your cousin thinks! But just because you two apparently don't hit it off, you're not going to use me as a stand-in for your hostility. Whether you intended it seriously or not, I'll thank you to remember it was still *your* suggestion that we come here!'

So intent had Gwayne been on making certain that Brad clearly understood her feelings on the matter that she didn't notice the figure which had suddenly appeared in the open doorway, but the sardonic tut-tutting which came in the momentary lull once she had finished had both their gazes flying in that direction.

The indolent stance of one shoulder supporting his weight against the door frame was now dismissed as the man moved into the room with a supple stride. 'Sounds as if you were well and truly being taken to task, old son,' he commented in a pleasantly controlled but somewhat mocking tone, a strong lean hand being extended towards Brad. 'Do you often find yourself on the receiving end like that?'

After only a minimal hesitation Brad clasped the outstretched hand briefly and then shook his head. 'Only once in a while,' he laughed in a rather forced fashion.

'But I have to expect that from a redhead, I suppose. How are you, Regan?'

During their exchange Gwayne took the opportunity to study Brad's cousin covertly. So this was Regan Fairfax, the owner of this beautiful homestead and—as they had discovered from their chat with his aunt—the great Fairfax grazing empire. She could more readily understand now why Brad had made his last infuriating remark, because his cousin was strikingly attractive, with that innate brand of vibrant masculinity which was both tempting and provoking at the same time.

His tall muscular figure seemed to dwarf Brad as they stood facing each other, and beneath the almost jet black hair his clear smoky grey eyes came as something of a surprise against the deep mahogany of his skin, but it was the slightly mocking tilt to the corners of his firmly curved mouth which signalled the greatest danger in Gwayne's estimation. There was a definite message to be read there, she mused, and it boded ill for anyone foolish enough to underrate this man, or the air of authority which seemed to envelop him like a second skin.

She was brought out of her contemplative reverie by Brad slipping an arm about her slender waist and pulling her closer against his side. 'Anyway, I guess I'd better introduce you two. Regan Fairfax, Gwayne Peters ... *my* girl,' holding her even more tightly to him.

It wasn't the first time Brad had used such a term to describe her and it had never worried her before, but as Gwayne's fingers came into contact with Regan's and she caught the taunting gleam in the depths of his cool eyes, she experienced a strong flare of resentment for Brad's possessive emphasis which had obviously been meant as a 'hands off' warning for his cousin, but which she found embarrassing in the extreme. Not even in her wildest flights of fancy could she imagine someone of Regan Fairfax's standing being interested in a parentless nonentity like herself, and she had no doubts that the look in his eyes had been created by the private amusement that Brad could have been so mistaken as to believe otherwise.

Regan relinquished her hand slowly, purposely, so it appeared to her. 'I'm pleased to meet you, Gwayne, and I hope you enjoy your time out here.' One dark brow lifted enquiringly. 'Have you ever been to the outback before?'

'No, no, I haven't,' she returned stiltedly, feeling unaccountably unbalanced in the face of his undoubted virility. 'Although I have been looking forward to rectifying that omission, however.'

'As long as you remember to keep that fair skin of yours well protected. A severe case of sunburn is not only extremely painful, but it can make you very ill as well,' he advised levelly.

Immediately his cousin had departed after a few more pleasantries were exchanged Brad turned on her irately. 'Why didn't you tell him to mind his own business? He's got no right telling you to keep your skin protected!'

'Then why didn't you tell him so while he was still here?' retaliated Gwayne tartly, pulling out of his grasp. 'Besides, his is the ultimate responsibility and it would be his staff required to look after us if we weren't well. He probably only mentioned it because they have more to do than play nurse to a load of thoughtless visitors.'

'Oh my, aren't we considerate all of a sudden? One meeting with the great Regan Fairfax and she's already championing his every word,' he jeered.

Gwayne rubbed the tips of her fingers wearily across her forehead. They had had a long day travelling and she really didn't feel like an argument to finish it off.

'Oh, don't be so touchy, Brad,' she pleaded with a sigh. 'I think we're both more than a little tired and it seems ridiculous to be fighting over something so trivial. Can't we just forget your cousin for a while and try to make our holidays as pleasant as possible?'

Straight away he was all remorse and back to his normal self as he reached for her hand, their fingers linking automatically. 'I'm sorry, honey. You're right, we are both tired, and I've been taking out my frustrations on the last person in the world I would want to argue with,' he grimaced crookedly, ruefully. 'We'll go and have a drink with Aunt Charlotte in the sitting room before dinner, shall we? Maybe that will revive our flagging spirits.'

The spacious sitting room was a delight to the eye with its brown studded calf leather sofas and chairs; original prints decorating the cool-coloured walls above the cedar wainscoting; matching Regency wall cabinets of coromandel wood; a Sheraton china cabinet which housed a large collection of both natural and polished Australian gemstones, and an assortment of small tables adorned with bowls and vases of dahlias, carnations and sweetly perfumed frangipanni.

As prospecting had been one of the major factors governing their coming to the outback, and as Brad's aunt hadn't as yet joined them, Gwayne headed interestedly to view the collection of gemstones once Brad had provided them both with drinks from the trolley standing between the wall cabinets. When Donna and Warren discovered them only minutes later they were already deeply engrossed in the colourful display.

Being the two novices to the hobby of gem-collecting,

Gwayne and Donna needed to rely on the men's knowledge to identify some of them such as the almost translucent rose red rhodonite, the peacock blue azurite, and the mint green chrysoprase. The opals, sapphires, emeralds, rubies, amethysts and diamonds they could distinguish for themselves.

With one forefinger wavering between a huge cabochon of black opal which was brilliantly exhibiting every colour of the spectrum, and a glittering square-cut emerald of magnificent proportions, Donna queried disbelievingly, 'Are you telling me that those are the sort of stones we're hoping to find while we're here?'

'Uh-uh, not quite, neither of those two come from around this district,' said Brad, and laughed at her crestfallen expression. 'We're far more likely to find some of these others.' He directed their gaze to different samples in the collection. 'Amethyst, aquamarine, garnet, beryl, malachite, moonstone, zircon, jasper, chert . . .'

'Heavens, don't confuse me, that sounds plenty to be going on with,' she grinned in return, eyes wide and expressive. 'Just point me in the right direction and let me at 'em!'

'It's not quite that simple, love,' put in Warren, chuckling. 'First, we need to find some promising locations.'

'Well, Brad should know those already,' she suggested reasonably. 'After all, he's apparently done quite a lot of fossicking on the station from time to time.'

'That's true, but most of the places I covered were in company with my mother and Aunt Karen and, believe me, once those two fanatics had been through an area you could usually say goodbye to any chance of your finding something worthwhile afterwards. They were nothing if not thorough,' Brad informed them wryly.

'Then we'll be breaking new ground, so to speak?' probed Gwayne, and received an emphatic nod of confirmation.

'I hope so. The thing is, of course, that someone else may have picked the area clean years before without us being aware of it. When Aunt Karen was alive the family often had parties of gemmologists and lapidaries camping on the property.'

'Well, they couldn't possibly have covered every inch of it ... it's too damned big,' decided Donna positively, bracingly. 'There must be somewhere that's relatively untouched. Why don't you ask your cousin? He might be able to give us some ideas.'

Warren endorsed the proposal with an approving wink. 'Good thought,' he grinned. 'That could save us hours or even days of wasted effort.'

'Or we could ask your Aunt Charlotte. Perhaps she could help too,' Gwayne put forward helpfully, sensing Brad's unspoken aversion to Donna's original suggestion.

'Mmm, maybe.'

He didn't sound very convincing, but before they could carry the discussion further Charlotte Fairfax herself hurried into the room, casting them all an apologetic smile.

'Goodness gracious, you must think me a dreadful hostess,' she began regretfully. 'Not there to greet you when you arrive, and now leaving you to have your aperitifs on your own. I do apologise, my dears, but it was quite unintentional. I became caught up with a minor household problem.'

Brad poured dry sherry into a delicate crystal goblet and handed it across to her with a soothing smile. 'Don't worry, Aunt Charlotte, we were well occupied ... admiring,' there was only the slightest hesitation before the word, 'the Fairfax Display. Gwayne and Donna have never been prospecting before.'

She sank down on to one of the leather sofas with a reminiscent laugh. 'Then I do hope you make some good finds. There's nothing more exhilarating than unearthing a gem of prime colour and quality, and nothing quite so depressing as a day spent digging in the hot sun without a single find to show for it.'

Gwayne could well imagine that to be the truth. 'You've done a fair amount of prospecting yourself, then, Miss Fairfax?' she enquired.

'In my time,' the older woman replied with a pleasurable nod. 'But not since my sister-in-law Karen died. She was the driving force where I was concerned, I'm afraid. Regan still goes out occasionally, but these days he doesn't really have the time to go as often as I suspect he would like to.'

'And the opals and emeralds? Did your sister-in-law find those too?' Donna asked, waving a hand back towards the cabinet.

'The emeralds, yes,' Charlotte nodded. 'One time when my brother had business in Western Australia and Karen went with him for a couple of months so she could hunt over the old fields and mines. The opals, however, have been in the family since the turn of the century. When they first discovered the black opal it took quite a long time for it to gain any popularity whatsoever—something it seems hard to credit, I know, when nowadays the best stones are more valuable than diamonds—but fortunately for us that didn't deter one of our ancestors from mining them, or retaining possession of those he discovered.'

Gwayne sipped absently at her drink, her thoughts slipping off at a tangent. How nice it would be to be entrusted with an article—not necessarily of commercial value—which had been handed down from generation to generation, and which would give one that sense of being a link in the family chain. Of belonging!

That was what she had always found hardest to come to terms with at the orphanage. That feeling of having been cut adrift, of being totally alone and without anyone with whom she could claim even the most remote kinship. A single entity in the midst of a pluralistically-orientated society. She didn't even have the right to call her surname her own because her mother—at least that was who they presumed had left her at the home—had pinned only a short note to her shawl informing them of her first name and begging them to take care of her for two weeks, after which time they would be able to return for her.

Of course they never had. The weeks had turned into months and then years, but still no one came to acknowledge her presence, and Matron had eventually provided her with a surname instead. Naturally enough under the circumstances there had been no consideration given to adoption—just in case—and so she had stayed on at the orphanage far longer than most of the other children and it had become the only home she had ever known.

CHAPTER TWO

DINNER, in the silk-lined, emerald velvet-upholstered dining room, was an ordeal as far as Gwayne was concerned. From the moment Donna had been introduced to their host she had set out to captivate him—not so blatantly that Warren could guess what she was about, for Donna was a natural charmer in any case, but certainly pointed enough for Gwayne to feel extremely uncomfortable in view of her friend's previously stated intentions. Then as the meal progressed, there were Brad's either moody silences or needling remarks to try and gloss over, or ignore, and what she could only term as Regan Fairfax's deliberately provocative comments to intercept. Whether he felt as strongly about his cousin as Brad obviously did about him she couldn't have said for certain, but one thing had become patently clear. That in his unusually aggressive frame of mind, Brad was no match for his supremely self-controlled relation, and the longer dinner lasted the more evident the fact became.

By the time coffee was served on the verandah Gwayne already had the beginnings of a headache and was in no mood to accept any of Regan's taunts with a courteous show of civility, and especially not when they came in the form of amused observations like,

'Your words with Brad earlier must have upset him more than you intended. He was like a bear with a sore head all through dinner,' as he came to lean against the rail beside her.

A sharply indrawn breath—whether to put a brake

on her ridiculously accelerating pulse, or because of the sheer ingenuousness of his suggestion, Gwayne didn't give herself time to decide—and she sent him a heavily sardonic look.

'But not because of anything I said ... as you well know,' she denied hotly and, when a glance over her shoulder showed Brad to be occupied in waiting for his aunt to pour his coffee, went on to demand, 'What were you trying to prove, Regan? That Brad's no match for you when it comes to mealtime repartee?'

His firmly contoured lips quirked lazily. 'Was I doing that?' he quizzed. 'I was under the impression I was being remarkably tolerant in fending off his rather ill-mannered belligerence.'

'Most of which you purposely initiated!'

Under his satirical regard Gwayne flushed rosily.

'Come off it, sweetheart, you know damned well that's not true. Brad was looking for an argument from the moment we entered the dining room.' One dark brow lifted fractionally, whimsically. 'What would you suggest I should have done? Allowed him to indiscriminately spoil everyone's meal?'

'I—well ... no, not really, I suppose,' Gwayne shook her head slightly. He wasn't entirely wrong in what he said. 'But did you have to be quite so sarcastic about it? Brad's been uptight enough as it is since we arrived.'

'So what's new?'

The baldly mocking question sent a deep crease furrowing across Gwayne's forehead and her eyes searched his for some sign that he was joking. When none was forthcoming she queried hesitantly,

'Are you trying to suggest that Brad's often like this when he's here?' in a tone of disbelief.

'Something like that.' The fascinating tilt to his mouth came into play again, disturbing the even tempo of her breathing and momentarily scattering her thoughts.

'But—but why?' she managed at last.

Regan took his time before answering, first drinking some of his coffee and then giving a broad-shouldered shrug. 'I rather think you would do better to ask him that.'

'Possibly,' she conceded, albeit a trifle doubtfully. 'But right at the moment I'm asking you.'

'Then don't.' It was an order no matter how casually said. 'You might not appreciate my reply and Brad definitely wouldn't thank me for infringing on his privileges.'

'And that worries you?' She foolishly allowed a slightly gibing note to enter her voice.

'Not in the slightest,' he dismissed the idea offhandedly. 'I've never yet found Brad to be a particularly disturbing opponent.'

Confronted by such cool self-assurance and recalling Brad's 'patronising' comment, Gwayne felt an abrupt need to display some defiance and sarcastically opened her eyes wide.

'Because he doesn't have your social connections and therefore isn't worthy of your concern?' she taunted, and was awarded an even more aggravating glance in return.

'No, because he allows his misplaced emotions to dictate his arguments instead of his head. The same as you're doing. The two of you must make a good, though somewhat volatile double!'

'But nevertheless still not good enough to cause *you* any consternation,' she just had to retaliate, her chin rising to a challenging angle.

'Nothing could do that,' interposed Brad, hearing the last of her words as he finally came to join them. 'Don't you know that Regan's never on the losing side ... of anything!'

'I can believe it,' she nodded wryly.

'I can't,' Regan refuted with a laugh, his eyes agleam. 'After all, Brad's the one with the beautiful companion tonight. In my book that makes me the loser.'

The pleased expression on Brad's face wasn't echoed on Gwayne's. She wasn't experiencing his sense of victory at all. In fact, her only feeling was one of rising anger that Regan should be deliberately furthering Brad's stupid notion that his cousin might be interested in herself, and she glared back at him stormily.

'Which is a circumstance I'm sure you could remedy in a very short time if you wished, and without having to resort to the company of someone like myself, a mere nobody from an orphanage and one of the world's unwanted!' she scoffed.

'A condition which no doubt underwent a dramatic reversal once you reached maturity.'

It was the raking appraisal which accompanied his words as much as the statement itself which sent the colour racing over Gwayne's cheeks, and in an effort to dispel the discomfiture which threatened to overwhelm her she fell back on flippancy as a means of protection.

'But naturally,' she smiled airily. 'Now it's a case of beating off would-be admirers with both hands.'

'Including Brad?'

'That's my business, not yours!' For a moment her rebellion showed.

His only response, however, was a provoking smile which had Gwayne catching at her breath and then Donna was claiming them from the table with an imperative,

'Come on, you three, come back and join the rest of us!' And to Regan, 'We have some questions that badly need answering. Like ... where's the best place for us to start searching for some gemstones which will make our eyes light up with awe when we discover them?' she sparkled outrageously.

Regan was the first to reach the table and made himself comfortable in the seat next to the brown-haired girl who wasn't bothering to hide her admiration as she gazed at him coquettishly.

'Well, there's always Yellow-Top Ridge and Amethyst Creek,' he replied to her question after some consideration, and promptly had Donna breaking in with a commending,

'Mmm, the second one sounds promising. Tell us more!'

He grinned at her obvious enthusiasm, but before he could continue Brad had interrupted,

'Surely they must have been worked out by now! There've been enough people go over them.'

'I agree you'd think so, but amazingly it seems there are still finds to be made,' their aunt now joined in the conversation. 'Why, only last year while mustering the sheep out Regan found the second largest piece of amethyst that's ever been discovered on the property. Didn't you see it when you were looking at them all inside?'

'I did wonder where it had come from,' Brad admitted, 'but I thought you might have found a deposit elsewhere.'

Charlotte moved her head negatively. 'No, but perhaps you'll be able to do that while you're here. The north end of the creek has seen very little activity and it was towards there that Regan made his find.'

'We would have to make a very early start in the morning and take one of the Range Rovers,' Brad immediately began planning the trek in his own mind.

'Otherwise we wouldn't make it back before midnight. As it is, it would be long after nightfall before we returned anyway.'

'Just so long as you remember to take a first aid kit, plenty of water, and all the necessary spares and equipment with you,' Regan reminded him.

'Don't worry, I'm not that much of a raw recruit,' Brad retorted swiftly. 'I have planned these trips before.'

'But, unfortunately, not always successfully!'

Brad's skin reddened beneath his tan as he became the focus for everyone's attention. 'All right, all right! So I wasn't fully prepared last time,' he shot back at his cousin resentfully. 'How was I to know the damned radiator hose was going to split on me?'

'Checking it before you leave has always proved as good a way as any,' he was informed on a highly caustic note, and it was only the timely appearance of Regan's overseer requesting his presence that prevented the situation from becoming an even more inflammable one.

In his absence Gwayne quickly reverted the conversation to their original topic and they soon had Brad's aunt racking her brains for other locations which might prove suitable for their endeavours. By ten-thirty all four of them were finding it difficult to keep their eyes open after the almost sleepless hours of the night before, and as Regan hadn't put in a reappearance they bade goodnight to Charlotte Fairfax and began making their way to their separate pavilions.

Considering she hadn't expected to sleep all that well— there had certainly been some revelations that day for her to think deeply about—Gwayne lost consciousness the moment her head touched the pillow, and although she awoke early the following morning she felt surprisingly refreshed and anxious to make a more detailed inspection of the homestead and its environs.

Presently, after washing and dressing in flared bottle green denims and a white cotton knit top, she checked and found Donna still sleeping soundly and then ventured out on to the verandah. Overhead the sky was a deep blue, as yet unfaded by the golden disc which was edging higher above the horizon with each passing minute, and in the distance the incessant chatter of a flock of elegant quarrions could be heard, while closer at hand the pink wings and glowing crest of a Major Mitchell cockatoo were discernible against the silvergrey foliage of the acacias on the opposite side of the lawn. Somewhere a dog barked, and was immediately silenced by a male voice, then from the rear of the house came the sound of gentle laughter as the house girls went about preparing breakfast.

It was all so very different from what she was used to that Gwayne didn't quite know where to begin her explorations until something cold and wet pushed against the toes of one foot in their open sandal and, with a visible start, she found she was being tentatively investigated by a sleek-coated puppy. He obviously wasn't very old, the unsteady state of his legs proved that, and with a murmur of pleasure Gwayne caught him up in her arms, to his apparent contentment, and proceeded down the steps.

'We'll have to see about getting you back to your mother, my lad,' she spoke softly to him as she followed the path beneath weeping pepper trees and sweet-smelling bauhinias to the back of the house. 'Perhaps that was her calling for you earlier.'

The pup gave a tremendous sigh and burrowed his nose deeper into the crook of her arm, making Gwayne smile as she stroked his smooth head and looked about her with wondering eyes. On her right was a precision-marked tennis court complete with shaded chairs and seats for relaxed spectating, and on her left an inviting blue-tiled swimming pool where the water iridescently reflected the rays of the warming sun, the surrounds of which were dotted with banana chairs and a redwood table supporting a brightly striped sun umbrella. Between the two the lawn sloped away from the house towards a tree-lined boundary beyond which the roofs of numerous other buildings could be seen.

As she stepped out across the grass Gwayne's lips curved wryly. When Brad had mentioned that his cousin owned a property out west she had never suspected it might be something like this! With her background she had always thought that this was the type of homestead you saw in photographs or read about, not one where you ever expected to be a guest. Not that she considered their way of life at the Ramsay Home for Children had been under-privileged. It just hadn't quite prepared her for the slightly overawing magnificence of Fairfax Downs!

After passing through the gate leading out of the gardens Gwayne hesitated, mentally tossing up between a cluster of cottages and the many outbuildings as the most likely venue to produce her tiny burden's parent. In contrast to the quiet sleepiness enveloping the homestead, here it seemed a hive of activity with stockmen moving back and forth across the compound, the sound of childish voices raised high as they greeted another day with exuberance, and the soft expectant whinnying of horses about to receive their morning rub-down and rations.

Her decision made, Gwayne moved along a well beaten track towards the first of the houses and then stopped, one hand shading her eyes against the glare as two men rode into the yard and dismounted by the stables. She recognised one of them as Regan immediately. Even though they were both dressed much the same in bush shirts and fawn drill pants, there was something about him which would make it impossible to mistake him for someone else, even amongst a crowd, she mused absently. Apparently her presence hadn't gone unnoticed either, because as a dark-skinned man led their mounts away they both raised fingers to the brims of their hats in acknowledgment, Regan's companion then saying something which brought ready smiles to their faces.

A sixth sense told Gwayne the amusing remark had concerned herself in some way and, with her face burning at the thought, she gave only the barest of nods in return and showed them a stiff back as she spun about and continued on her way.

Suddenly she wasn't alone any more as Regan matched his long-legged stride to hers. 'Ah, I see you've found him.' His glance dropped to the bundle in her arms. 'Young Carl will be pleased. He was most upset when he discovered the pup was missing.'

Gwayne stroked a finger beneath the velvety jaw, her eyes remaining on the small form. 'He found me, actually ... on the verandah.'

'That was quite a distance for him to travel,' Regan smiled, and then advised, 'Here, this way, he belongs in the last house,' with a guiding hand being laid on her arm which she promptly shrugged off and earned herself a drawling, 'Don't tell me you're still annoyed because of what I had to say about Brad last night?' in retaliation.

She lifted one shoulder uncaringly. 'You're entitled to express your opinions the same as anyone else!'

'Thanks!' His tone was so dry it almost crackled. 'But if you're not naturally an early riser there's no call for you to feel obliged to change your habits while you're here. We didn't expect to see you surfacing for quite a few more hours yet in any case.'

Now Gwayne's eyes sought his, suspiciously. 'Meaning?'

'You don't appear to have slept too well,' he enlightened her lazily. 'Or are you just temperamental by nature?'

It was becoming harder not to be and she rounded on him resentfully. 'No, I am not! I just don't happen to like jokes being made at my expense. At least, not those in which I'm given no opportunity to share!'

'Jokes at your expense?' She had the satisfaction of seeing him frown and immediately pressed home her advantage.

'That's right! It *was* something about me that you and your friend found so amusing back there, wasn't it?'

Recollection feathered its way over Regan's face and his mouth shaped into a smile which had Gwayne's heart pounding dramatically against her ribs. 'That was no joke, sweetheart. It was a compliment!'

'Oh?' warily, and not a little doubtfully.

'Uh-huh! Dan reckoned it was amazing what good taste Brad could show in some instances.'

There was a particular nuance in his voice which threw Gwayne instantly into embarrassed confusion, but fortunately for her there was help near at hand in the shape of the chubby four-year-old who was hurrying along the path towards them.

'You found him, you found him!' His joyful cries reached them long before he did. 'You found Lonely!'

'Is that his name?' Gwayne grinned as she went down

on her haunches in order to hand back his errant pet. 'After this morning's effort I should think that's very appropriate.'

Dark blue eyes peered out from beneath a tangle of golden curls. 'What's that mean?' he queried dubiously.

'Only that Miss Peters thinks you chose the right name for him, Carl,' Regan reassured him before cautioning, 'But until Lonely is old enough to find his own way home again I think you'd better make sure it's not so easy for him to get away.'

Carl hugged his furry treasure closer to his T-shirted chest and nodded solemnly. 'I'll keep him in a drawer in my room, then he won't be able to.'

Gwayne had difficulty in not showing her amusement at his solution to the problem. 'Oh, but that would make Lonely and his mummy sad because they wouldn't be able to see each other,' she tried to explain, and guessing that it wasn't likely to appeal to Carl's mother either.

'No, I should leave him in his box in the laundry and just put a board across the doorway if I were you,' Regan now added his persuasions to hers. 'That way everyone can get in, but Lonely can't climb out.'

The suggestion obviously found merit in Carl's eyes because a happy smile began to spread across his youthful features. 'I'll ask my daddy to do it now,' he told them determinedly, and without further ado he was scampering back the way he had come with the puppy precariously clutched in both hands.

'Lonely?' Gwayne queried once the child had disappeared through his front door and they had started back up the track.

'He was the only one in the litter, so Carl thought he might be ...'

'Lonely,' she supplied for herself with a laugh.

But a laugh which faded abruptly when she found Regan's grey gaze concentrated disturbingly on her soft lips and causing an uncontrollable shiver of purely physical awareness to chase down her spine. It was the first time in her life that she had experienced such a starkly primitive feeling, and that it should have been directed towards Brad's cousin gave her extra cause for dismay. Ever since their initial meeting she had been aware of Regan Fairfax's compelling attraction, but she had certainly never anticipated finding herself in the position where she would want to respond to it quite so willingly. For a moment her long lashes fanned down to hide the self-condemnation in her eyes. The atmosphere between Brad and his cousin was tense enough already without her adding fuel to the flames!

'Have you always been an orphan, Gwayne?'

Regan's question burst in upon her meditations without warning and caused her to look up at him with a bewildered frown.

'I'm sorry, what did you say?'

'I said, have you always been an orphan?' he repeated. 'Or can you still remember your parents?'

'No, I never knew them,' she shook her head regretfully, surprised he should have remembered that one passing reference from the night before. 'Well, I suppose I knew them at one time, or at least one of them. It was always presumed it was my mother who left me at the home, but,' her head tilted sideways in consideration, 'it could just as easily have been my father, I guess.'

'Your name is a rather unusual one for an institution to bestow, isn't it? Or did they prefer the unfamiliar?'

She shrugged indifferently, but avoided giving a

direct answer all the same. 'No, they mostly made use of the ever-populars like Elizabeth, Anne, and Margaret.'

'But not in your case?'

'I—I already had a name before—before I arrived.'

Regan opened the gate for her to precede him into the garden and then closed it, his smoky grey eyes surveying her steadily. 'How would they have known that if they weren't even aware of the sex of the person who left you with them? You apparently weren't old enough to tell them.'

Throughout her life everything had always seemed to hinge on that note which had been left with her and the promise it had contained. An unfulfilled promise which still had the power to hurt unbearably if she dwelt on it for too long.

'Oh, look! Isn't it beautiful!' The chance flight across the lawn of a lone bird, resplendent in its glorious lime green, emerald and scarlet plumage, gave her the opportunity to hopefully distract his attention and thereby change the subject. 'What type is it?'

'He's a red-winged lory,' Regan supplied levelly, then caught her completely unawares by tipping her face up to his to enquire, 'Don't you like to talk about your early years, Gwayne?'

'I—why should it worry me?' she countered, pulling away from his touch as if she had been burnt. 'I've got nothing to hide. At least, I don't think I have,' with a nervously forced half laugh.

'Then why don't you answer my question as to how the orphanage knew your name?'

Trust him to return to the heart of the matter! She tried another tack. 'Because it's none of your business! I'm not giving you a third degree regarding *your* origins, am I?'

'Be my guest,' he drawled.

Although it was a decidedly tempting invitation to find out more about him, Gwayne put a firm clamp on her wayward inclinations and directed her annoyance with herself towards him instead.

'I don't have to. I reckon I can make a fairly accurate guess without asking a single question,' she retorted caustically. 'You're an only child who was doted on by your parents, who only went to the very best schools, and who only mixes with the very best people ... normally! And at a guess I'd say that's where I come in,' she continued sardonically. 'I'm a novelty. In your lofty sphere you don't usually come across specimens like me and it amuses you to pull me apart to see what makes me tick. The more so probably because I also happen to be Brad's girl-friend and, as the two of you obviously don't see eye-to-eye on anything, then you might also be lucky enough to pick up something which you can use against him!'

Regan ran a hand around the back of his neck in utter disbelief. 'Hell! You really like to underestimate yourself, don't you, sweetheart?' Followed by a dry, 'Come to think of it, you didn't do a bad job on me while you were about it.' Then, 'But you're wrong on just about every count! I am not an only child—I have a sister who's a year younger than myself and who's married and living in W.A. I did go to boarding school, I admit, but only because for secondary schooling this far west we don't have much other choice. As for mixing with only the best people, as you put it, well, that rather depends on your definition of "best", doesn't it? If you're meaning the admirable, praiseworthy, salt of the earth kind, then maybe I do. But ... just to set the record straight and rid you of all those preconceived misconceptions of yours,' his voice turned several degrees cooler and his glance was one of piercing steel, 'it has never been my practice to judge a person's worth by the amount of money they happen to possess! I prefer to leave that sort of misjudgment to Brad and others of his kind!'

'And just what was that remark meant to imply?' she demanded. She had really stirred up a hornet's nest this time.

Regan swung his gaze away towards the homestead and expelled a deep breath. When his eyes met hers again the anger had been replaced with pure mockery.

'You don't know your boy-friend very well, do you, Gwayne?' he taunted.

'Which is no answer at all!'

'But all you'll get from me.'

'Because you're only interested in putting doubts in my mind which, as I said before and I noticed you didn't dispute, thereby gives you a chance to get at Brad through me?' she gibed.

A deep laugh issued from the bronzed column of Regan's throat. 'Sweetheart, I don't need you to get at Brad. Or haven't you noticed the ample opportunities he generously gives me himself to do that?'

Which was something she couldn't really deny, not if she was to be completely honest, and she bit her lip despondently. It was like being trapped in a crossfire and not knowing in which direction to flee. Towards Regan spelt danger in large capital letters for her peace of mind, but at the same time her allegiance to Brad was being badly strained by his disturbing attitudes. All in all, it was far from being a promising state of affairs, she sighed.

They had almost reached the homestead before Regan spoke again and Gwayne could hardly believe her ears when she heard him questioning as if there had been no interruption,

'What else did the note tell them besides your name?'

She glared at him furiously, her turbulent thoughts now finding the outlet they had unconsciously been seeking. 'Oh, God, are you back to that again? Who said there was a note anyway?'

'It was a simple matter of deduction,' he relayed lazily. 'It had to be either that, or a telephone call, but as you said the staff at the orphanage weren't sure of the sex of the person who left you there, then it had to have been a written communication.'

And she'd thought that subject was safely behind her! She should have known better than to have minimised his powers of perseverance. After all, to survive successfully in the outback that was one quality which was required in abundance, and that the Fairfaxes had done just that had never been in doubt!

'Okay, so you've very cleverly worked out there was a note,' she smiled acidly. 'Why should it interest you?'

'Because you intrigue me. I keep getting the feeling that I know you from somewhere.'

Gwayne made a mocking grimace. 'Maybe we shared an elevator one time when you were in Sydney.'

'Oh no!' he vetoed decisively. 'Strangely enough I do know it wasn't that transitory.'

'Then it must have been my double,' she quipped. 'But it certainly wasn't me.'

'No,' he agreed slowly, 'but have you considered that it may have been a relation of yours? An aunt, a cousin ... your mother?'

Gwayne felt the tension mounting inexorably inside her as Regan's speculations took shape, but it was that last insinuated kinship which had her backing away from him with her hands clenched at her sides, her eyes blazing brightly.

'Damn you, Regan Fairfax, for being so persistent!' she railed, and too distressed to mind her language. 'What right have you got to make such a lousy assumption? Couldn't you have just let things be?'

'For crying out loud, why?' Both his hands snaked out to grasp her wrists, pulling her back towards him. 'Aren't you interested in finding out if you have a family? In finding your mother even?'

'No, I'm not!' she flung back at him fiercely. 'Why should I be? She wasn't interested enough in me to ...'

'Go on,' he prompted, his eyes watching her carefully. 'To ... what?'

'To come back for me, if you must know! She promised faithfully she would collect me within two weeks!' she blazed, unmindful that her struggles to be free were raising red welts on her soft skin where he was holding her so firmly. 'And now that you've heard the whole pitiful story, I hope you're satisfied! Does it make you happier knowing I'll never forgive you for bringing it up again after I'd managed to ignore it for so long? For reminding me how much my mother *cared*!'

'Of course it doesn't, you little idiot!' Regan shook her urgently. 'But there's a host of possibilities which could have prevented her from keeping that promise. She may have ...'

'Oh, don't bother listing them, I've heard all the excuses there are on offer before,' she broke in contemptuously. 'She could have flown to the moon too, but it's far more likely that she just couldn't be bothered because I was too much of a nuisance!'

He gave a snort of disgust. 'Personally, I'd like to get my hands on the fool who told you about the contents of the note in the first place! What the hell were they thinking of to burden a child with such information?'

'Don't you say anything against Mrs Coleman, it wasn't her fault,' Gwayne immediately came to the defence of the orphanage's Matron. 'There was a couple who wanted to adopt me when I was about five and she had to explain to them why they couldn't.'

'There was still no reason for her to tell you.'

'She didn't,' Gwayne sighed. 'It was some of the older kids. They overheard the three of them talking in the office.'

Releasing his hold at last, Regan moved a hand to smooth a silky lock of hair back behind her ear in a curiously soothing gesture.

'And is that why you feel obliged to deprecate yourself all the time? Because you've never had anyone to tell you how much you mean to them, to make you feel of value?'

There was a timbre in his voice which turned Gwayne's bones to jelly and in a desperate effort to counteract it she gave an unsteady laugh.

'Amateur psychology yet! You've got me all figured out, haven't you, Doctor Fairfax?' A taunting look from beneath her lashes and she mocked, 'Do you prescribe treatment as well?'

'I know the remedy I'd like to recommend, sweetheart, but I suspect Brad wouldn't approve,' Regan advised softly. 'At the moment I rather think he'd consider that was his province.'

His meaning was plain and Gwayne dropped her gaze rapidly as her cheeks began to burn with discomfort. The trouble was, part of her embarrassment was due to the fact that his insinuation didn't appal, as it should have done, it appealed. And strongly at that!

'Yes, well ...' She licked nervously at her lips and

ran her hands down the side of her denims. 'Some cures can be more painful than the ailment.'

'But not if administered in the correct dosages,' he drawled with a lazy piquancy which was Gwayne's final undoing.

'I—I wouldn't know, so I'll just take your—your word for it,' she stammered.

Right at the moment she was willing to agree to almost anything in her desire to escape, and Donna's appearance on the verandah couldn't have been more opportune.

'Have you had breakfast yet?' the other girl called out to them.

'No, we're just coming for it now,' Gwayne replied thankfully, quickening her steps, and not waiting for Regan to accompany her.

CHAPTER THREE

BREAKFAST was a more informal affair than dinner had been the night before, with everyone helping themselves from the various warming trays which lined the richly polished sideboard. Never a big eater in the mornings, Gwayne bypassed the meats and eggs which their male companions were consuming with obvious enjoyment and settled for some toast, marmalade and coffee instead.

'How about you two having your first riding lessons today?' Brad suggested to Gwayne and Donna once they were all seated at the table and, after they had both returned pleasurably expectant nods, he asked of his cousin, 'You do have a couple of mounts suitable for beginners, I hope, Regan?'

'And one for a not quite experienced rider too,' Warren put in with a laugh because it was some years since he had sat a horse.

Regan nodded equably. 'I think we should be able to accommodate you easily enough. Just ask Sam to saddle up Puppet, Angel and Beau.' He turned to Warren to advise, 'Beau's a stallion but an unusually even-tempered one. You won't have any trouble with him.'

'That's good,' Warren grinned. 'I wouldn't like to display my incompetence too much by spending all of my time remounting.'

'Is it accepted as a matter of course that you're going to take a few tumbles when you're learning then?' enquired Donna, her expression a little more dubious now.

'In most cases,' Brad corroborated with a ruefully reminiscent smile. 'Although, even riders with years of experience have to be prepared to take a fall now and again. It's a hazard which comes with the occupation.'

'I'll bet Regan doesn't, though. Do you?' Her brown eyes swung admiringly towards the man at the end of the table.

Gwayne watched covertly as one broad shoulder lifted fractionally higher. 'I wouldn't exactly say that,' came the wry response. 'I guess I've had my share of broken bones over the years, the same as everyone else.' He was honest if nothing else, she was forced to admit.

In acknowledgment Donna half laughed, nervously. 'You're not making me feel any better, either of you,' she complained.

Warren hastily swallowed a mouthful of steak and shook his head. 'Stop letting it worry you, love. You can't come to much harm at a walk, and I expect that's all you'll be doing today.'

'Is it?' she promptly asked Brad, and was given a reassuring affirmative.

'Just about. Unless you get the hang of it quickly and feel you want to tackle the trot and the canter.'

'Oh, that's all right then,' Donna sighed with relief. 'We'll be happy to keep it at that for a while, won't we, Gwayne?'

Since riding was an accomplishment Gwayne had long respected, and envied, the lessons couldn't proceed fast enough to her way of thinking, but in view of Donna's apparent anxiety she felt it would hardly be tactful to say so at present and answered non-committally.

'By the way, Brad, unless you're planning to make

the trip out to Amethyst Creek towards the end of your stay, I might suggest you do it within the next few days,' Regan now advised. 'With the shearing starting next week it's more than likely we'll be needing all available vehicles from Friday onwards for mustering.'

'Hmm, I hadn't thought of that,' Brad mused thoughtfully as he finished pouring his coffee. 'What about we go tomorrow, then? That suit everyone?' His glance took in his three fellow guests.

'Yes, sure. We're looking forward to it,' Gwayne answered for all of them.

'Right! Then we'll have to see Mrs Wallace some time today about having some food and drinks packed for us, as well as checking out the vehicle. Which one of the Range Rovers can we take, Regan?'

'You'd better make it the most recent model, there'll be less likelihood of you striking trouble.'

'Why don't you come with us too?' Donna proposed gaily. 'Miss Fairfax was only saying yesterday that you didn't have many chances for prospecting. Surely this is the perfect opportunity.'

As she heard the invitation Gwayne's startled gaze left the piece of toast she had been buttering and flew apprehensively towards the end of the table. Heavens, let him refuse, she pleaded mutely. She found his vital presence far too disquieting to be able to envisage a whole day spent in his company with anything even approaching detachment!

'Some other time perhaps, thanks, Donna.' She heard Regan decline the other girl's offer and let out her breath on a sigh. 'We've got a busy time ahead of us and at the moment it's all hands to the wheel.'

'Well, if we can help in any way don't hesitate to give us a yell,' Donna smiled. 'You have only to ask and we'll come running.'

Gwayne looked at her friend in something close to dismay. Whatever did Donna think she was doing? It was becoming painfully obvious that she was trying to attract Regan, and she said as much to the other girl once they had finished breakfast and were heading for their rooms to change into more suitable gear for riding.

Donna's only reaction, however, was to shrug unconcernedly. 'There's nothing wrong in letting a man know you're not averse to his company. Regan's my kind of man and I have no intention of pretending he isn't.'

Regan was every woman's kind of man, Gwayne admitted ruefully, but only to herself. To Donna she suggested, 'And what about Warren?'

'Well, what about him?' Another shrug and Donna glanced at her slyly. 'Besides, you didn't seem to be caring too much about Brad this morning when *you* had Regan all to yourself.'

'But—but that's ridiculous!' Gwayne exclaimed, her colour rising. 'I could hardly refuse to walk back from the yards with him.'

'Why go down there at all ... unless you wanted to accidentally bump into him?'

Gwayne shook her head exasperatedly. 'Now you're really letting your imagination run away with you. The only reason I went was to see if I could locate the owner of a puppy which I found wandering on the verandah.'

'And it was this puppy, I suppose, that left the marks on your arms which were so visible when you returned?'

'No, that was Regan,' Gwayne retorted sardonically. 'I was so eager to show him how I felt about him that he had to grab hold of me to protect himself.'

Donna's brown eyes resumed their normal gay

sparkle. 'Okay, okay, you're getting through to me that I'm on the wrong track,' she grinned. 'So how did you get those marks? Which, incidentally, Brad must have been blind not to see.'

'I know,' Gwayne pulled a thankful face. 'But luckily he was fully occupied with other matters.'

'The marks—don't forget the marks,' urged Donna irrepressibly, and Gwayne laughed.

'All right, I'm coming to those. We had a—a difference of opinion, I guess you could call it, and he was determined I was going to stay and listen to his views, whether I wanted to or not.'

'It must have been something important for him to go to those lengths.'

'He apparently thought so.'

'You didn't, though?' Donna questioned alertly.

'Obviously!' was the very dry retort. 'For some unknown reason he was interested in probing into my background at the orphanage, or more particularly, the method of my arrival there.'

'Oh-ho!' Donna's exclamation carried a wealth of meaning. Having been friends with Gwayne for a couple of years now she knew better than most just what sort of reaction such an unwanted interest was likely to produce. 'And did he also say *why* he was interested?'

Gwayne shrugged. 'Something about thinking he knew me from somewhere. Which, of course, he doesn't.'

'No, you would have remembered him if you'd met before, wouldn't you?' Donna was only stating the obvious and Gwayne didn't deny it.

'More than likely. His isn't a personality you could forget in a hurry.'

'Or would want to.' Donna had the last word as they

reached the doorway to Gwayne's room. Then, 'I'll see you in a few minutes, okay?'

An agreeing nod and they parted company, Donna continuing on to her bedroom and Gwayne entering hers with a frown puckering her brow, her thoughts hopelessly entangled as she reached for and lit a cigarette.

First and foremost there were the hurtful recollections concerning her parents' desertion to attempt to lay to rest once more—something which had frustratingly always caused her problems—and secondly, the alarming thought to overcome that she was unconsciously allowing Regan's provocative attraction to get under her guard. A senseless situation considering the difference in their backgrounds; her relationship with Brad which she had been quite content with up until now; and last, but by no means least, the fact that at thirty-four Regan was clearly in no hurry to change his way of life and form any lasting involvements.

Almost as if on cue to remind her of another complication, Donna could now be heard whistling softly to herself in the bathroom, and Gwayne's mouth curved wryly. If her friend wanted to make the most of her opportunities while she was here that was her business, but Gwayne had no intention of joining the ranks and competing with her for the doubtful honours to be gained from such actions!

When the girls reached the yard Brad already had their mounts saddled and immediately handed them each a wide-brimmed hat similar to the ones that he and Warren were wearing.

'Here, you'd better put these on,' he advised with a grin. 'We don't want you looking like a couple of boiled lobsters by lunchtime.'

'Huh!' Donna wrinkled her nose at him and thrust

hers on to the back of her head. 'I've got a feeling that's going to be the least of my worries,' as her gaze measured the height of the animals mistrustfully.

'Not that way, idiot,' Warren exasperatedly decried the angle of her headwear and promptly pulled it forward into a more suitable position. 'It's not there as a decoration, you know, it's for protection!'

Donna suffered his ministrations goodnaturedly as Gwayne settled her own hat into place and then Brad was handing them each a set of reins together with the advice, 'We'll walk them to the paddock and start your lessons down there. It's a good level area and it's nicely grassed at the moment.'

'To break our falls?' Gwayne's winged brows rose expressively as she slipped into step beside him, the brown gelding she was leading keeping close by her shoulder.

'I hope not. I think Donna's almost ready to call the whole thing off as it is.' He looked across at her speculatively. 'You're not, though, are you?'

'Not likely!' Gwayne rubbed her hand down the muscles of the shining brown neck beside her and smiled happily. 'I don't care how many spills I have. I want to learn to ride, and as quickly as I can.'

'Well, you've certainly got the right attitude,' he approved. 'Just make certain you don't try to get ahead of yourself, that's all, because that's when you're really likely to come a buster.'

'Yes, teacher.' She managed to look duly chastened, but only until a wayward thought intruded. 'Although didn't both you and Regan say that all riders have to be prepared to bite the dust occasionally?'

'Sure we did,' he conceded emphatically. 'And the more experienced you are the worse your falls are usually, because then it's not just a case of you losing your balance and slipping off at a sedate pace, but quite often it's a matter of your horse coming down at the gallop and taking you with him. Remember, this country isn't composed of gently rolling green hills; it's rough and it's rocky, and it's strewn with hidden obstacles. Accidents can happen to anyone, but I don't intend that one should happen to you because your desire to progress isn't matched by your ability.'

'That's telling me!' Gwayne made a rueful moue. 'Okay, you're giving the orders ... for now!' her eyes twinkled impishly.

Brad shook his head in mock despair. 'Witch! You'll be the death of me yet.'

But Gwayne wasn't listening, her interest had been claimed by the visual splendour spread before them as they rounded the last of the outbuildings and came face to face with the far-reaching open country. Today there wasn't the homestead to try and discern amidst the heat haze, nor was she tired, and so could drink in the scene with marvelling eyes. Gone were the siennas and ochres she had been conditioned to expect and in their place were the brilliant greens, yellows, reds and purples of the wildflowers which stretched as far as the eye could see. The land was alive and blossoming again, and its magnificence was close to taking her breath away.

'It's unbelievable, isn't it?' she murmured incredulously. 'I was expecting it to be so dry and brown and dusty.'

'As it will be again shortly,' Brad retorted quickly, and with an almost dour pleasure, it seemed to Gwayne. 'In the meantime, maybe it's just living up to its name in your honour.' He swept an arm wide to include the whole panorama, his expression distinctly mocking. 'The Plains of Promise! Named by the original Fairfax settler and upon which their not inconsiderable wealth is founded.'

'You seemed ...' She hunched one shoulder and sought the right words. 'Slightly envious when you said that.'

'Not envious, Gwayne, but bitter!' she was corrected stonily. 'All this should have been mine, not Regan's!'

Gwayne only just managed to swallow her astonishment in time so she could stammer out the query, 'But—but how?'

'Because it was *my* mother who introduced Karen to Michael Fairfax! It was *my* mother who dated him first!'

Was this really the cause of all Brad's animosity towards his cousin? Plain old-fashioned jealousy? Good grief, surely not!

'But what's that got to do with ...' she began, only to be cut off by a fiercely contradicting,

'It's got everything to do with it! You don't know what my Aunt Karen was like. Or perhaps you do, seeing that Regan's exactly the same,' acidly. 'But she wasn't like my mother—shy and unassuming—no, she was always the life of the party, the one with the brightest and most charming smile, the one with hordes of admirers, but who was never backward in adding another one to their overflowing numbers. Not even if that extra one happened to be her own sister's escort!'

'And if he hadn't wanted to be charmed then I very much doubt that she could have done so,' Gwayne unaccountably found herself defending Karen Fairfax.

Brad's face darkened ominously. 'Are you trying to say that it was my mother's fault? That she wasn't capable of holding him anyway?'

'No, that's not what I'm trying to say at all!' she hissed back at him, all too aware that if their voices rose any higher Donna and Warren would be able to hear every word. 'What I'm trying to get through to you is that your mother has always seemed more than content with her choice of husband to me, and that being so, I don't know what you're making all the fuss about! Besides,' she smiled wryly and attempted to bring a little lightness to the situation, 'have you considered that, had your mother married Michael Fairfax, then it's quite possible Regan could have been your elder brother and, as the younger son, you still wouldn't have owned Fairfax Downs?'

It was obvious Brad couldn't see the humour in her suggestion. 'No, that possibility hadn't occurred to me!' he snapped furiously. 'Regan has far too much of his mother in him for that to have been the case.'

'Just as you are your father's son?' Gwayne couldn't resist reminding him, because the similarities between the two of them were endless.

'If that's your idea of being funny, give it a miss!'

'It wasn't, actually. It was an attempt to put things into their proper perspective,' she told him sardonically. 'If Regan couldn't have been your brother because he's too much like your Aunt Karen, then by the same token, you could never have been a Fairfax because you're too much like your father!'

'You think it's all a bit of a joke, don't you?' he sneered.

Gwayne shook her head wearily. 'Not in the slightest. I'm finding it all rather distasteful, if you must know. Why can't you just be satisfied with the loving family you've got instead of worrying so much about what might have been? There's a lot of people who would be only too glad to have parents like yours.'

'Including you?'

'Yes, including me,' she admitted openly.

'I'm not surprised, I've often thought that was the main reason you've continued going out with me. You're more attracted to the family atmosphere of my home than you are to me,' he criticised.

'Oh, don't be so absurd!' Gwayne denied the suggestion immediately, although it did succeed in having her attempt to analyse her feelings towards him more closely all the same. An exercise which still hadn't been satisfactorily concluded by the time they reached the paddock where their lessons were to begin.

Understandably, conversations between Gwayne and Brad were rather strained during the remainder of the morning, his instructions being given in coldly autocratic terms and her replies in just as cool monosyllables. Not that Gwayne was overly concerned because she couldn't really believe that Brad's normal good nature wouldn't reassert itself sooner or later, while in the interim she was finding it to her advantage to be able to give her total concentration to what she was doing instead of making an effort to join in the men's conversations as Donna was doing—to her own detriment.

From the first moment Gwayne had swung on to Puppet's back and gathered in the reins she had felt balanced and completely at ease, whereas Donna, nervous even before they began, continually slid from side to side, her hands too high and tight on the reins in her needless anxiety to keep Angel at a walk.

'For heaven's sake, Donna, *relax*!' Warren exhorted for the umpteenth time, and received a positive glower for his pains.

'How can I when I keep slipping all the time? I've never felt so insecure in all my life! Personally, I'm beginning to think this horse-riding is overrated to blazes. Give me a car I can feel comfortable in any old time.'

'And I bet you didn't feel all that safe and comfortable the first time you sat in the driver's seat of one of those either,' he retorted. 'Give it a chance, love, you'll get into the way of it soon.'

'Hah, says you!' Donna pulled a disgruntled face at him. 'My seat already feels as if someone's given it a good going over with a broom handle.'

'Well, maybe it wouldn't if you stopped wriggling around up there so much.'

'Oh, shut up, Warren!' Her interest fast declining and her patience exhausted, Donna pulled her mount to a halt, stiffly eased herself down to the ground and proceeded to arch her back in relief. 'The way I feel now I wouldn't care if I never saw another horse again!'

Gwayne came to a stop beside them. 'Would you like to do something else instead, then?'

'No, that's all right.' Her offer was waved aside with a wry grin. 'You can keep going if you want to. I'll just wander around here and take the kinks out.'

'At least you didn't fall off,' Gwayne reminded her with a smile.

'Wonders will never cease!'

'Never mind, you'll probably do better next time.'

Donna's expression was hardly enthusiastic. 'If there is a next time. After this I think I'll stick to board riding for my feats of balancing, thanks very much.'

'Mmm, it is surprising your ability there hasn't stood you in better stead for this, isn't it?' Gwayne commented thoughtfully.

'Probably because I don't mind coming off in water. This ...' Donna dug at the earth gloomily with the toe of her shoe, 'isn't nearly so inviting.'

Now that she had confidently and rapidly mastered walking and turning properly, trotting was the next gait on Gwayne's agenda, but it involved such a different action that she knew immediately it was going to take far longer to graduate from this step than it had from the other. Brad's commands to 'go with him' were seemingly impossible to comply with when she always appeared to be coming down as Puppet was rising, so much so that eventually even she was glad when he advised that it was time they headed back to the homestead for lunch.

'Well, so you've been learning to ride, have you?' Charlotte smiled at the two girls as the meal progressed. 'How do you like it?'

'Speaking for myself, not very much, I'm sorry to say,' Donna grimaced lightly. 'Gwayne's going well, though. She took to it like a duck to water.'

'I don't know that I'd say that exactly,' Gwayne laughingly disparaged the flattering observation. 'Trotting's proving something of an obstacle.'

'You're not doing too badly if you're trotting already,' Regan's deep voice put in evenly. 'More often than not it takes longer than one morning to acquire the proper balance and control.' He turned enquiringly to Brad. 'How good is she?'

Having recovered from his previous outburst, Brad responded drily. 'Well, I'm no expert myself, of course, but I would have to say she's a natural! From the time she threw her leg over that horse's back she automatically did everything right. She sits right, she holds the reins right, and she's got perfect balance. What more can you ask of a pupil?' He shook his head in disbelief. 'I reckon she could have been trotting after the first half hour without too much effort.'

Gwayne sent him a reproachful look. 'Yet you kept me walking around in circles and doing figures of eight for hours!' she accused.

'I had to,' he countered unrepentantly. 'If only to make certain my eyes weren't deceiving me.'

The talk moved on to other matters, mainly their proposed trip for the morrow, with Brad and Warren arranging to check out the vehicle that afternoon—a decision which brought a look of utter tedium to Donna's face until, in answer to a question by his aunt, Regan mentioned that he intended using the other four-wheel-drive vehicle to check that the bore drains further out weren't becoming overgrown with the flourishing new growth, whereupon her expression underwent a startling transformation.

'Well, that certainly sounds more interesting than watching these two,' a waving hand indicated Warren and Brad, 'prepare a car for our outing. Would you mind very much if I went with you, Regan?' She sent him her most beseeching glance.

Of all the people at the table it appeared to Gwayne that Warren and Regan were the least surprised by the request—although she suspected for completely differing reasons—and promptly had her suspicions confirmed when she intercepted Regan's deeply mocking glance before he replied with a pleasant, but slightly sardonic,

'Not at all, you're most welcome. It hadn't occurred to me that you would find checking bore drains of interest.'

'Oh, well, everything about station life interests me,' Donna prevaricated rapidly. 'And it will be a chance to see more of the country, of course.'

Gwayne could feel herself going red on her friend's behalf. Couldn't Donna see for herself that Regan

knew exactly what was going through her mind? Or
had she become so infatuated that she didn't care any
more? As for Regan Fairfax, she could quite happily
have thrown something at him! He clearly wasn't interested in Donna—didn't he already have a girl-friend
by the name of Arleen somebody or other, anyway?—
but at the same time he was making absolutely no effort
to discourage her flirtatious advances.

'How about you, Gwayne? Would you care to come
too?'

So deep in her own thoughts had she been, Gwayne
visibly started when the object of those thoughts spoke,
but when her gaze rose to his it wasn't surprised, it was
angry and defiant.

'No, thanks,' she refused abruptly. 'I may be able to
give Brad and Warren a hand in some way, or failing
that, I might resume my riding practice.'

She didn't know why he had seen fit to issue her
with an invitation to join them, but whatever the
reason she wasn't about to help him further it. He had
accepted Donna's request to accompany him, now he
could put up with the results. And if that meant having
to suffer her coy attentions for the whole of the afternoon it served him right!

As it turned out Gwayne's offers of help with the
Range Rover weren't required, so after being strongly
adjured to keep to what she had been shown, she set off
eagerly to collect Puppet and headed for the same
paddock they had used that morning. However, as she
passed out of the compound she came across Regan's
vehicle parked beneath a towering gum, a decidedly
vexed-looking Donna the only occupant.

'Hi, how come you're still here?' she asked in amazement. 'I thought you and Regan had left ages ago.'

'You mean Regan, *Les*, and me, don't you?' Donna

amended drily. 'He forgot to mention that one of his stockmen was coming as well! Next time I'll make sure that we're not going to have company before I invite myself on one of his trips.'

Gwayne could have said she had no one to blame but herself, but thoughtfully held her tongue in that regard, preferring to ask,

'Where are they, then? Aren't you leaving until later now?'

'Oh, Regan's overseer stopped us just as we'd got started. He wanted to see him about something and Les went with them. They said they wouldn't be long,' Donna relayed indifferently.

'I see.' A pause, and, 'Well, if you're not at all that keen to go now, why don't you tell him you've changed your mind? You could always say you'd decided to give Warren a hand after all.'

'Come off it, that would be tantamount to telling him outright that I only suggested going in the first place because I thought there would only be the two of us!' When there was no answer she continued shrewdly, 'You believe he already knows that, don't you?'

Gwayne shrugged unhappily. 'He's no one's fool, Donna! Anyway, with his looks and money I'd hazard a guess and say this isn't the first time he's been the hunted rather than the hunter.'

'And Regan Fairfax is one of those males who like to do their own chasing ... right?'

'In simple terms, yes.'

'Oh, well, there's no harm done,' Donna grinned crookedly. 'I still figure I've got nothing to lose by trying.'

It was impossible not to admire her tenacity of purpose and Gwayne began to smile, her perfectly even

white teeth gleaming, her sherry-coloured eyes twinkling merrily. As soon as she saw Regan approaching
them, however, her amusement disappeared as quickly
as it had come and by the time he reached their side a
look of wary defensiveness had replaced it.

'Sorry to have kept you waiting, Donna,' he apologised with a smile that set Gwayne's senses on fire. 'Les
should be along in a minute and then we'll be off.' His
right arm shot out and caught hold of Puppet's bridle
as, after a surreptitious finger wave to her friend,
Gwayne began to slide away. 'And if you're going out
to practise on your own, sweetheart, pay close attention to what you're doing. Okay?'

'Don't worry, Brad's already been to great lengths to
impress on me what I'm allowed and not allowed to
do.'

He nodded approvingly and then inclined his head
to enquire, 'How are you trotting, by the way?'

'Uncomfortably at the moment,' ruefully.

'Understandable, although not quite what I meant,'
he laughed. 'I was meaning, with or without stirrups?'

Gwayne's eyes widened in astonishment. 'With, of
course!'

'Then try it without,' he suggested with a grin. 'It's a
good exercise in balance and it will make you sit well
down in the saddle. Just make sure you keep your
stirrup leathers crossed over in front of you, otherwise
if one bumps into him he'll think it's you signalling
him to move faster.'

Lovely thought, she grimaced inwardly, even though
she could see the logic behind his suggestion. With no
stirrup irons to push against she would have no choice
but to move with her mount.

'All right, I'll give it a go,' she decided. 'It couldn't
possibly be worse than what I was doing this morning.'

'As long as you remember to keep those stirrups well clear.'

Gwayne nodded and began moving away, anxious to try this new method, and shortly afterwards she heard the vehicle start up and head out in a westerly direction.

That afternoon was one of the most frustrating—but still enjoyable—that Gwayne had ever spent. She began by slowly refreshing herself with those stages she had already been through and then progressed gradually to trotting, first with the stirrups and then without. She noticed that this latter style had the effect of making her bump more when she rode, but it did put a stop to her and Puppet's mid-air collisions, and when she switched back to using stirrups the next time found she had a far better feeling for his movements, although she still wasn't as proficient as she would have liked to be.

The hours passed quickly and it wasn't until she saw the returning Range Rover darkly outlined against the setting sun before it disappeared behind the stores building that she realised just how late it was. Leaning forward to pat the gelding's satin-smooth neck, she couldn't refrain from releasing a soft murmur of protest. She was feeling distinctly stiff and sore herself now, and decided it was time they too returned to the homestead.

Confident she could ride him back to the yards without anything untoward happening, Gwayne reached for the crossed stirrup leathers in front of her and thoughtlessly let them fall back into place instead of carefully repositioning them as she had done each time earlier in the afternoon. She knew immediately what she had done wrong, but unfortunately Puppet gave her no time to do anything about it. With his own eagerness to reach his stable at this hour to guide him, he presumed those two thumps against his ribs were advising him to make haste and obediently bounded forward into a gallop.

Caught with the reins in one hand only and her feet struggling to find the stirrups, the outcome was inevitable. In an attempt to pull him up Gwayne put too much tension on the right rein and he began to wheel; consequently, as he went one way, she went the other. With the ground rushing up to meet her she momentarily recalled Brad's advice about taking the brunt of the impact on her forearm, but in the short space of time allotted her automatic reflexes overcame the reasoning and an outstretched hand took the full force of her fall, sending red-hot shafts of pain spearing upwards from her wrist to her shoulder.

She lay still for a moment trying to recover her breath and her composure, then gingerly made it to her feet. Well, nothing seemed broken, she mused wryly, although her wrist was still complaining about its treatment in no uncertain terms. Bending, she retrieved her hat, brushed it against the side of her leg to remove the pieces of grass clinging to it and settled it back on her head prior to walking across to where Puppet had halted as soon as they had parted company.

'We certainly finished the day with a bang, didn't we, feller? Or at least I did,' she half laughed ruefully as she began leading him stiffly towards the paddock gate. 'But I won't be making that mistake twice, I can tell you! I shall let those leathers down in one-inch steps next time.'

Puppet pushed his head up and down against her shoulder as if he understood every word she was saying and together they made their slow laborious way back to the yards, where Gwayne was extremely grateful to be able to hand him over to Sam for unsaddling and grooming because by then her wrist felt like a raging inferno and it was all it could do to support her hand, let alone have any weight put on it.

'How did you go?' an unmistakable voice queried as she left the yard as hurriedly as possible and headed for the house.

She half turned and raised one shoulder deprecatingly. 'All right, I guess. I'm still in one piece.' Just!

'But a fairly sore and sorry piece, I should say, by the way you walked out of the yards a moment ago,' Regan smiled as he caught up to her and tilted her pale face up to his with a finger beneath her chin. 'Give it a rest for a couple of days, sweetheart. It doesn't pay to overdo it.'

'No, I suppose not.'

It was easy enough to agree when there was no chance of her doing any more riding anyway until her wrist recovered, but in the meantime she did wish he would quicken his steps a little. He was moving even more slowly than she was and it seemed to be taking them an age to reach the garden. She would have liked to have nursed her wrist in her good hand too in an attempt to relieve some of the pain, but she reluctantly decided against it. Having been stupid enough to temporarily forget his advice was bad enough, but she wasn't going to willingly place that stupidity on display, and especially not to Regan of all people.

At last they came to the gate and Regan swung it wide for her, but as Gwayne passed through their attention was distracted by a kookaburra breaking into a sudden burst of laughter and the rebounding gate slapped against her injured wrist, bringing unbidden tears to her eyes and an involuntary yelp to her lips.

Now she had a reason to support her arm and she did so gratefully, deliberately avoiding Regan's intent gaze as it swept over her suspiciously.

'Okay, what happened?' he demanded.

Her eyes flew up to his watchful ones briefly and down to her arm again. 'Oh—er—nothing much really. The gate swung into me, that's all,' she tried to make light of it. 'I'm sorry I cried out like that, but I—I wasn't expecting it.'

'Don't lie, Gwayne, you haven't the colouring to do it successfully!' His voice wrapped around hers like the coils of a whip. 'I asked you what happened, and I wasn't referring to the gate!'

'I—I don't know what you mean,' she evaded uneasily. 'The gate hit my arm and it hurt. Maybe there's a piece of wire loose on it which dug into me.'

'Show me where,' he ordered, but Gwayne chose to ignore the outstretched hand which accompanied the command and shrugged dismissively.

'It's all right now, thanks. It's not even painful any more,' she lied.

'Like hell it's not, you're as white as a sheet!' he countered, steel-grey eyes raking over her savagely. 'Now, are you going to tell me, or are you going to force me to look for myself?'

Gwayne glared back at him resentfully. Only this morning she had accused him of being too persistent. She hadn't known the half of it!

'I only sprained it,' she finally confessed on an exasperated sigh. 'Nothing to make such a big deal about. It will probably be better by morning.'

'May I see it?'

She was still reluctant—at the thought of him touching her as much as anything.

His brows quirked ironically. 'There's nothing to be ashamed of in taking a fall. It happens to all of us sooner or later.'

If he thought to make her feel better he wasn't succeeding. Her unwillingness hadn't been brought about by the fall itself so much as by the foolishly inattentive cause, and in response she moved her head in a gesture which was neither an acknowledgment nor a dismissal, but holding out her arm defeatedly for his inspection.

Frowning at the slightly swollen shape, he promptly began to feel and test for a fracture with deft and experienced fingers, his touch as light and careful as possible, but still managing to make Gwayne wince on a couple of occasions before his thorough check was completed.

'Nothing broken, I'm pleased to say, but you'll need an ice pack to take that swelling out and a supporting bandage for the next few days,' he smiled down at her gently, releasing his hold. As they resumed walking he eyed her curiously. 'How did it happen?'

Gwayne shrugged wryly. 'I dropped the stirrup leathers too hastily and Puppet leapt into a gallop. When I tried to pull him up he started to turn ... but I didn't.'

'So couldn't you have said that before? Why all the secrecy?'

Because she hadn't wanted to appear so incompetent in his eyes? Gwayne retreated from that line of thought and answered diffidently.

'I don't know. Maybe the thought was in the back of my mind that after I'd forgotten such a simple and logical instruction, you might have considered I was too irresponsible to be allowed out again with one of your mounts.'

'And that worried you?' The corners of his mouth curved humorously.

'Well, yes, of course. I've always wanted to be able to ride and this seems my best opportunity of learning,' she explained quickly, just in case the question had been two-edged, as she half suspected.

'Then we'll have to do everything possible to make certain your ambition is fulfilled, won't we?'

The lazy smile which enveloped her had Gwayne's colour rising uncontrollably and her eyes seeking something else to focus upon. She felt herself becoming frighteningly vulnerable to Regan's essential magnetism and, in consequence, her answer was defensively snubbing.

'Oh, I think Brad should be able to do that well enough without you having to concern yourself, Regan,' she retorted. 'We wouldn't want to interrupt any of your work schedules.'

His dark head inclined to a mocking angle. 'That'll make a nice change!'

'How do you mean?' she questioned warily.

'I mean that somehow or other Brad usually manages to turn the station upside down at least once while he's here,' he reported sardonically. 'Last time, three years ago, we had to mount a search party and go looking for him when the Range Rover broke down. The time before that ...'

'Okay, okay, so he isn't as wise in the ways of the outback as you are. That's not surprising, is it? He doesn't live here.'

'Then it might be advisable if he, like you, accepted help when it was offered,' Regan recommended pointedly. 'It could make life just that much easier for all of us.'

'Meaning you're already regretting having allowed us to come?'

He sent her a heart-stopping look from beneath his thick lashes. 'Oh, I don't know that I would go so far as to say that,' he drawled. 'I have a feeling your stay is still likely to prove extremely interesting.'

'For whom?' guardedly.

'Well, for you, naturally,' he laughed. 'We wouldn't want you to have a bad opinion of our outback hospitality.'

Which, Gwayne was sure, wasn't what he had meant at all, but as she doubted further questioning would elicit a more direct answer she merely gave him a disbelieving stare and hurried up the steps on to the verandah.

'What about that wrist of yours?'

A hand settling firmly on the nape of her neck brought her to a halt when she turned in the direction of her room and she spun round haughtily.

'If you would just let go of me it would make it a lot easier to attend to it,' she smiled sweetly.

'But you happen to be going the wrong way. The medicine chest is in the office down there.' He indicated another of the breezeways.

Anxious to be gone from his unsettling influence, Gwayne shook her head decisively. 'I don't think I'll need the medicine chest, thanks all the same. I can fix it in my room.'

'With only one hand?'

Before Gwayne had a chance to reply he had already begun shepherding her down the passage to the door at the far end, requesting one of the house girls who passed them on their way to bring some crushed ice and some tea to the office.

'I could have asked Donna to help me,' she protested

angrily as they entered the neatly furnished room where a number of impressive graphs decorated two of the walls. 'There was no need to frogmarch me in here like some wayward delinquent!'

'Then stop behaving like one,' she was ordered irritably, and thrust on to a dark red leather-covered chair in front of the desk. 'While you're on Fairfax Downs you'll do as I say, and that especially applies where injuries are concerned!'

Gwayne contented herself with a mutinous but impotent glare. How could she do otherwise when only the night before she had defended him to Brad in just such a situation by saying that his was the ultimate responsibility?

It was Nora Wallace the housekeeper, stick-thin in contrast to her rotund husband, who arrived with the tray and who poured their tea from a wicker-handled bone china pot while Regan competently wrapped her arm within a cocoon of ice. Gwayne could immediately feel its palliative effect against her heated skin, and Mrs Wallace clucked sympathetically as she moved Gwayne's cup conveniently closer.

'There, you drink your tea and you'll feel much better,' she advised persuasively. 'Once the ice has done its work and your wrist's bandaged, you'll be as good as new.'

'I hope so, Mrs Wallace,' Gwayne replied with a faint smile, dropping her hat on to the desk and combing her fingers through her rumpled hair. 'It puts something of a damper on a holiday when you're disabled.'

'Oh, but it won't be for long. By this time next week it will all be behind you,' the housekeeper gave her a comforting pat on the shoulder as she headed for the door.

In the lull which followed her departure Regan

extracted two foil-wrapped Disprin from the steel chest sitting on the shelf behind him and handed them across the desk.

'Here, take these, they'll also help alleviate the pain,' he recommended brusquely, and lowered his eyes to the arm resting in her lap. 'How is it feeling now, anyway?'

'Better than it was, thank you.'

Gwayne's gaze collided with his cool grey one and wavered nervously. Her attempt to gainsay his authority as to which one of them should treat her injury obviously hadn't been too well received, she reflected. But perhaps it would at least give her a breathing space in which to rearrange her defences. Regan Fairfax at close quarters was an emotion-shattering force which she frustratingly seemed unable to disregard, even though she was wholly aware that such an attraction could only be to her own disadvantage.

She sighed and obediently swallowed the tablets before pointing to the ice pack and asking, 'How much longer will this need to stay on?'

Regan's glance lifted from the papers he had been idly inspecting. 'I hope not too long. Why? Is it uncomfortable?'

It wasn't, but *she* was rapidly becoming so. Damn him! Why should he be able to look so calm and self-assured when the tension-fraught atmosphere between them had her nerves quivering feverishly?

'No, not really,' she managed to answer his question impassively after taking a deep controlling breath. 'But I would like to know for how many hours I'm expected to sit here.' One arched brow peaked impertinently. 'Until dinner? For the rest of the evening? All night, perhaps?'

'All three if I think it warrants it.'

Gwayne's temper simmered—he was being deliberately difficult—and she retaliated stormily. 'You know something, you've had too much authority for too long!' she gibed. 'You've now reached the stage where you think you can order anyone and everyone around just as you please!'

His lips curved mockingly. 'And while you're on this property don't doubt that I can't, or won't, sweetheart,' he counselled arrogantly. 'Disappointing though you may find it, I can assure you I have no intention of waiving my control just because some of my decisions don't happen to suit you.'

'Or anyone else for that matter, I'm sure!' she returned sarcastically, her eyes sparkling brightly. Jumping to her feet, she made for the bookcase at the other end of the room. 'Well, as it looks like being a long night, I trust the idea of my improving my mind as I while away the hours isn't going to be seen as a direct challenge to your authority.' She flashed him a derisive look over one shoulder. 'I am allowed, I take it?'

Regan swept an arm wide. 'Help yourself,' he invited in a tone which sounded remarkably close to being amused, and once Gwayne had cursorily examined the titles lining the shelves she understood why.

'Don't you have anything other than books on accountancy or animal husbandry?' she demanded fractiously. She had hoped that with her attention occupied elsewhere she might have been able to forget his disturbing presence for a time. 'Surely you have some magazines ... or something!'

'Sorry, not in here,' he apologised without seeming the least apologetic, and she swung angrily back to the desk.

'Well, what am I supposed to do then to fill in the time? Assume the lotus position and meditate?'

'If that's what you wish,' he annoyingly took her at

her word. 'However ...' he paused and his eyes swept over her chaffingly, 'If you would care to stop pacing up and down like a caged animal, I could perhaps check to see how the swelling has reacted to the ice.'

Gwayne pressed her lips together tightly. 'It was impossible for you to have done that five minutes ago, of course!' she flashed.

'Not impossible, no, just impractical.'

A not very informative response, but Gwayne refused to ask him to elaborate. She had the distinct feeling that that was exactly what he wanted her to do, but she had no intention of leaving him an opening by falling in with his wishes. Instead she waited until he had carefully removed the wrapping and then queried, 'The swelling's gone, hasn't it?'

Regan felt the area with gentle fingers before concurring, 'Just about. I think binding will be all it will need from now on.' He turned to retrieve a bandage from the chest behind him and proceeded to fold it firmly around her wrist, securing it with a small hooked metal clasp. 'I would like to take another look at it some time this evening, though,' he continued, and gave her a long steady look. 'Also, I wouldn't advise you to go out with the others tomorrow. It's rough country out there and your arm would be better served if you rested it completely.'

'Oh, no!' Gwayne exclaimed. 'I was looking forward to going and—and it is only my left arm, after all. I can do whatever needs to be done with my right hand.'

'And if you need both hands?'

'Now you're just being hard to get on with,' she complained, her chin lifting to a defiant angle. 'But you don't have to worry, I won't be taking any unnecessary chances with it. I've no wish to be one-handed for any longer than I absolutely have to.'

'You're determined to go, then?'

'Yes—yes, I am.' It seemed ungrateful after his thoroughness in attending to her, but she couldn't see what possible harm could befall her if she took reasonable care. Tentatively, she put out a conciliatory hand. 'I—I would like to thank you for your treatment, though. It does feel much easier now,' she half smiled gratefully.

A muscle moved tautly at the side of his jaw. 'Consider it part of the service,' he shrugged.

Gwayne picked up her hat and began moving slowly for the door. Now that she wasn't being detained she perversely found herself reluctant to leave.

'Yes, well, I—I guess I'd better be getting a move on otherwise I won't make it in time for dinner,' she murmured inconsequentially.

Regan merely nodded an impersonal endorsement, and with a vexed sigh for her own contrariness Gwayne slipped out of the room and began hurrying along the verandah.

CHAPTER FOUR

It was only just light when the four of them departed the following morning, their spirits high with the thought of the finds they might be fortunate enough to unearth. Leaving the homestead perimeter behind, they turned north and while the going was still reasonably good Brad kept his foot down on the accelerator, knowing that before they finally reached their destination there would be some extremely slow driving to be done over less agreeable terrain.

As the Range Rover thrust steadily onwards Gwayne gazed out at the subtly changing landscape with appreciative eyes. She felt as if she had suddenly been plucked away from everything that was familiar and deposited in the middle of some strange and colourful new world. Wherever she looked there were wildflowers in profusion. They carpeted the rolling plains and climbed inexorably over the burnt orange sandhills—acre upon acre of pale pink desert roses, purple emu bushes, golden yellow everlasting daisies, magenta parakeelyas, large green pussytails, and the unforgettable brilliance of the red and black desert pea. It was a sight guaranteed to dazzle the most jaded of eyes, and Gwayne's certainly weren't that. The Plains of Promise! Aptly named, and richly rewarding to those with the boldness and perseverance to bend it to their will and claim it as their own.

Brad eased the vehicle into a lower gear and edged it slowly through the waters of a shallow rock-strewn watercourse and up on to the opposite bank. The sun was well above the trees now and the temperature inside the vehicle, as well as out, was rising relentlessly.

'How about we stop for a moment and have a drink while I take another look at the map?' he proposed, halting beneath the low branches of a black box tree. 'From here it's all new country to me too.'

'You mean we're about to fearlessly blaze our own trail?' Donna grinned as she began filling their mugs with chilled fruit juice from one of Mrs Wallace's flasks, and after Brad's absent nod of confirmation as he and Warren pored over the detailed sheet of paper in his hand, 'Well, I hope you're better at reading a map and a compass than I am. I wouldn't fancy getting lost out here.' She turned to Gwayne. 'You don't seem to notice it so much while you're on the move, but now ...' she paused and her gaze swept round in a semi-circle, 'it makes you realise just how alone you are, doesn't it? Look at it all!' she exclaimed with an out-flung hand extended towards the horizon. 'Miles and miles of absolutely nothing, and no one. Not a thing's moving except us. There's not even a breeze to rustle the leaves on this tree. It's eerie!' she shivered involuntarily.

Gwayne took a refreshing mouthful of her drink and licked at her lips slowly. 'I think it's heaven! There're no car tyres squealing, no voices arguing, no sirens, no horns, no rattles, clangs, or crashes,' she sighed contentedly. 'And there's plenty of things moving out there if you look hard enough. He's wide awake,' she shaded her eyes with her hand and pointed out a brown falcon as it soared on an air current high above them. 'And there's a kangaroo giving itself a good scratch beneath that cluster of trees by the bend in the creek. There's also an emu keeping a most suspicious eye on us from those bushes opposite, and unless I miss my guess, there's quite a few sheep making themselves comfortable in the shade of those coolibahs over to your right.'

'Well, who would have thought it?' Donna pulled a laughing face for her own lack of observation. 'It's obvious I'm no nature-lover, isn't it?'

'Only because you were too occupied in worrying about the lack of human habitation.'

'Ah, but you must admit that none of those you mentioned would be of much help if you were lost.'

'I don't know about that,' Gwayne disagreed rapidly. 'I believe it's possibe to find water by watching the flight of some types of birds. Not flesh-eaters like him,' she indicated the falcon again, 'because they apparently get most of the moisture they require from their prey, but wild pigeons and finches are said to be very reliable indicators. And of course, sheep and kangaroos don't usually travel all that far from water. Bob Evans, in the office, was telling me when he discovered we were coming out west that if you follow fresh grazing animal tracks downhill they'll lead you to water.'

'Downhill!' Donna hooted. 'He's got to be having us on! Except for a few outcrops the whole area is as flat as a tack!'

'Yes, well, it certainly looks that way, doesn't it?' Gwayne started to chuckle with her. 'I don't think I would like to be in the circumstances where my decision as to which way was downhill might mean the difference between life or death.'

'Me either!' the other girl endorsed her comment with feeling.

'You two ready to continue our trek?' Warren called, draining the last of his drink and replacing his mug in the hamper. 'Brad reckons it will take us another hour or more before we get there.' His face creased into a broad teasing grin. 'Provided we don't miss any of the landmarks, that is.'

'Beast!' Donna brushed past him with a mock-ferocious glare. 'You heard us talking about that, didn't you?'

'You're not worried that we'll lose our way, are you, honey?' Brad asked as he slipped an arm about Gwayne's shoulders and walked back to the vehicle with her.

She shook her head and smiled. 'With a map *and* a compass we shouldn't have any trouble.'

'As long as he knows how to read them correctly,' teased Warren incorrigibly, and had them both making threatening gestures towards him.

Shortly they were on their way again, the country becoming more rugged but no less fascinating as they bounced and jolted further northwards. In the distance great ridges of granitic rock stood out like fiery beacons as the sun's rays slashed across them, and where spinifex and roly-poly clung tenaciously to hard-won footholds. Detouring around a steep-sided gully Brad swung his head briefly to give the two girls in the back an encouraging smile.

'According to Regan's directions the north arm of Amethyst Creek is in the lee of those ridges up ahead, so it shouldn't be too long now,' he said.

Gwayne wiped the back of her right hand over her forehead and grimaced wryly. 'Just as well, I think my blood's on the point of boiling.'

'Mine too,' sighed Donna. 'If there's any water left in that creek I might turn this into a swimming expedition instead.' She leant forward to tap Brad on the shoulder and enquire, 'Will it still be running?'

'Sorry, I wouldn't know what the creek's like this

far north,' he half smiled ruefully. 'It might be, or it could have degenerated into a string of waterholes. Then again, it could be dry altogether by now too.'

Donna groaned and sent Gwayne a speaking glance. 'Comforting, isn't he?'

'Mmm,' she laughed. 'Still it will be something just to get out of here.'

'I'm even beginning to have my doubts about that,' her friend retorted, lifting her hair gratefully from the back of her neck. 'There doesn't appear to be many trees up ahead for shade.'

Three-quarters of an hour later they were all tumbling out of the Range Rover in relief after Brad had managed to locate a convenient patch of shade formed by a jutting rock. The few low-growing trees there were either too close to the crumbling edge of the creek, or else incapable of giving any protection. The water level in the surprisingly deeply bedded gully, however, was almost non-existent. Only two meagre waterholes were all that remained in their particular section—much to Donna's disappointment —the rest consisted of a dry rocky channel which meandered out of sight around the next ridge after a couple of hundred yards.

A short walk along the bank, searching for the most convenient way down the sharp slope, had them unanimously deciding on a route near to the largest of the water-filled basins, and while Brad and Warren returned to the vehicle to collect their equipment, Gwayne and Donna began the somewhat precarious descent.

All went well for the first few feet until Donna, who was in the lead, suddenly found herself confronted with a savage-looking, though harmless, stumpy-tail lizard which had been sunning itself on the rocks. With a startled gasp she flung herself backwards out of its path, but in doing so knocked Gwayne completely off balance and sent her stumbling helplessly.

Before she inevitably lost her footing altogether, Gwayne's mind had started working at a furious pace. She knew that if she fell forward her already injured wrist would take a lot of extra punishment which it wasn't in a condition to resist and, with Regan's warning about needing both hands ringing dismally clear in her brain, she made a last-ditch effort to protect it. She deliberately allowed her feet to slip away from under her and skated down the rest of the stony bank on her back—straight into the waiting water-hole at the bottom.

Attempting to catch her breath, she lay for a moment exactly where she had landed, and wondered whether she had any skin left on her back at all. It certainly felt raw! Above her she could hear Donna calling out agitatedly.

'Oh, Gwayne, I am sorry. Are you all right?' The sound of frantic scrambling coming closer and then a louder, 'Gwayne! Are you all right?'

Slowly she inched herself into a sitting position and lifted a hand in acknowledgment. 'I think so,' she grimaced, and experimentally moved the fingers of her left hand. 'At least my wrist is still okay.'

'But your poor back!' Donna ejaculated as she eventually made it on to level ground. 'You've ripped your shirt to pieces!'

Gwayne shrugged and immediately wished she hadn't when it felt as if her back had been stabbed simultaneously with a score of red-hot needles.

'Forget the shirt,' she recommended dryly. 'How's the skin underneath it?'

After a careful inspection Donna asked, 'You want me to be honest?'

'Is it *that* bad?' Gwayne's brows arched expressively.

'Quite frankly, it's a mess! Although there is some good news.'

'Such as?'

'I don't think there's too many really deep cuts. Mostly they seem to be surface ones only.'

'What on earth are you sitting in that water for?' Brad's amused voice sounded from the top of the bank, and levering herself stiffly to her feet, Gwayne turned to quip,

'Because I felt like cooling off, of course! Why else?'

Donna shook her head vigorously in denial. 'No, she didn't, she fell ... and her back is a mass of cuts. You'd better make sure you bring the first aid kit with you, Brad, when you come down.'

A shocked, 'Hell!' and he disappeared from sight. Reappearing a few minutes later with Warren close behind him and a red and white box tucked under one arm, he made a rapid descent.

'You're okay otherwise, Gwayne?' he queried worriedly as soon as he reached her.

Allaying his fears with a smile, she nodded. 'Pretty much.'

'How did it happen?'

'I'm afraid it was my fault,' Donna was already explaining before Gwayne could answer. 'A lizard startled me and I cannoned backwards into Gwayne, making her lose her footing.'

'Well, these things happen, I guess, but now we'd better get it fixed up as soon as possible.' He handed the kit across to Donna, advocating, 'You're probably the best one to attend to it,' and began taking off his shirt which he then gave to Gwayne. 'Here, you'll need something to keep the flies and the sun off,' he smiled. 'And once that's done we'd better start heading back to the homestead.'

'Oh, don't be silly!' Gwayne waved his proposal aside quickly. 'I'll be all right once we've put something on it. It's too far to have come not to get some enjoyment out of it now we're here.'

'But it would hardly be an enjoyable day for you,' Donna pointed out, frowning.

'Of course it will, and who knows?' she grinned. 'I may even make the biggest find of all time in compensation.'

'You're sure?' questioned Brad and Warren almost in unison.

'I'm sure.'

Brad exhaled heavily. 'It's your decision, I suppose. As long as you let us know immediately if it feels like it's getting worse,' he cautioned.

The matter settled, Gwayne and Donna found a handy spot for their purpose while Brad and Warren began an inspection of the creek bed in the opposite direction.

'At least I'm cool from the waist down now,' Gwayne grinned, looking at her soaked jeans as Donna helped to strip off her shirt and bra. 'I'm only sorry it didn't have ten feet of water in it instead of two.'

Donna didn't answer, she was too busy frowning over what she was seeing, but once she had managed to wash away the dirt which had been clinging to some of the deeper abrasions and had applied a soothing salve, it didn't look quite so bad. However, she still felt she had to ask,

'Gwayne, are you really sure you wouldn't rather go back to the homestead? Even with that ointment on, it must still be horribly painful.'

Easing herself gently into Brad's shirt—she had decided against wearing her bra because of the friction—Gwayne again gave a veto.

'No, honestly, it's much better now,' she insisted, then laughed. 'I just hope I'm not becoming accident-prone, that's all. If I continue at this rate I can see myself going home in a wheelchair when our four weeks are finished!'

Donna gave an expressive shudder, ordering, 'Don't say things like that!' as she re-packed the medicine kit and they wandered back to where the men had left the rest of their things. After bending to put the first aid equipment and Gwayne's clothes away, she came upright rubbing her hands together gleefully. 'Now! How do we go about unearthing all these fabulous gems?'

When the men returned from their foray they were only too willing to put her enthusiasm to good use and for the next few hours Gwayne and Donna found themselves diligently scouring the deposits in the creek bed for crystals of the attractive amethyst. It was a long laborious process with most of their time spent either on their knees or their haunches, and particular attention had to be paid to any hollows, bars, or curves where the current would have momentarily been blocked, as these were the most promising locations. Meanwhile, Brad and Warren were making just as thorough an exploration with geological hammers and chisels of the rocks lining the banks, searching for a glimpse of the violet quartz being weathered from its parent formation, and hunting for geodes—rounded rock masses—which might have the desired crystal lining.

Auspicious the area may have been, generous it was not, at least not to them that morning, and by lunch-time their only discoveries had been a few pieces of jasper and chert. Nice enough specimens to be polished, Warren had advised, but nothing to get excited about.

'I'm beginning to understand what your aunt meant when she said there was nothing so depressing as digging in the hot sun and finding nothing,' Donna remarked to Brad with wry feeling as they sat in the shade beside the four-wheel-drive eating their meal. 'Besides which, I ache from top to toe from all that bending. Goodness knows how Gwayne must be feeling.'

As three pairs of eyes concentrated upon her enquiringly, Gwayne's lips curved into a rueful grin. 'As if I'm never going to be able to straighten my back again!'

'Would you prefer it if we gave this afternoon a miss, seeing we've had no luck so far?' Brad offered helpfully.

Her sherry brown eyes glinted with a teasing light. 'Not unless everyone else wants to. You're not going to use me as your excuse for returning home early. I've stuck it out this long, another few hours won't make much difference.'

'Spoilsport!' laughed Warren, and had them all chuckling.

As soon as they had cleared away the remains of their meal they were back hunting along the creek, only towards its source this time. Disappointingly, this proved less rewarding than their earlier efforts had been, with not even a piece of common jasper to their credit until the girls came across an old rotting tree trunk wedged diagonally across the channel and began digging into the gravel which had accumulated against it.

'*Look!*' Donna almost screamed in her excitement. 'I think I've found some. Well, it's the right colour,' she added as an afterthought.

Warren was the first to reach them, dragging a

magnifying glass from his shirt pocket as he came. 'That's it all right,' he confirmed with a grin. 'Although it's not a terribly good sample, it has a few defects.'

'I don't care, I'm still going to keep it,' Donna laughed happily.

'Even so, you could still have it polished and made up into a piece of jewellery if you wanted,' Brad advised after he too had inspected the one-inch hexagonal formation. 'It's just that you can't facet them when they carry flaws.'

'In that case, let's get back to work and find some that can be!' Donna dropped down on to her knees with more eagerness than she had shown for some hours. 'There's just got to be more down here somewhere,' she forecast fervently.

But for all their digging and sifting only a few worthless fragments were uncovered before they reached bedrock and, eventually, with their expressions mirroring their disappointment, they were forced to call it a day. The hour was already later than they had intended and now they hurried to re-load the Range Rover so they could put as many miles as possible behind them before the light faded altogether.

The trip back to the homestead was a prolonged and agonising nightmare for Gwayne. Not that she had mentioned it to the others, but during those last hours they had been prospecting her back had grown progressively more and more painful. Because of the heat the salve had dissolved in some places, permitting Brad's shirt to adhere to her lacerated skin and making it sting sharply whenever she moved too abruptly. What made it worse was the fact that she couldn't even steady herself against the jolting by leaning back in her seat as she had done on the outward journey, but had to try and keep upright the whole way.

'Almost there,' Donna leaned across and squeezed her arm consolingly as the welcoming lights of the homestead made an appearance at long last. 'You'll feel better once you've had something to eat. It's hours since we had lunch.'

Gwayne smiled faintly. Eating was the farthest thing from her mind at the moment. All she wanted was a hot bath to soak the shirt from her back and to fall into bed. The bruises she had suffered during her fall were also beginning to make themselves felt in no uncertain manner now and she had more aches and pains than she could ever remember having at the one time in her life. As far as she was concerned, the faster she could climb into bed and lose consciousness the better she would like it.

It took Gwayne an age to alight from the vehicle once they pulled up at the rear of the house and even longer to traverse the verandah with Donna after Brad and Warren had left to seek their own pavilion with the advice, 'We'll let Mrs Wallace know we're back, and we'll see you in the dining room in about thirty minutes.'

Turning on to the front verandah, Gwayne drew in her breath keenly on discovering Regan and his aunt, together with an unknown but extremely fashionably dressed young woman of some thirty years, seated around the table drinking coffee.

Charlotte Fairfax noticed them first and smiled warmly. 'Oh, good, you're back. Did you have any luck?'

'A little,' was Donna's quick reply as she eagerly unwrapped her prize from the cloth she had been carrying it in and handed it to the older woman, barely answering when Regan introduced them both to Arleen

Halford, the glamorous blue-eyed blonde at his side, because she was too anxious to explain, 'Warren and Brad did say it is flawed, but I still think I'd like to have it polished.'

'Whatever for?' Arleen's pencilled brows rose sardonically as she ran ring-encrusted fingers affectedly over her sleek pageboy-styled hair. 'What earthly good is a stone with a defect in it?'

'Well, it's—it's ...'

The question had obviously taken her friend by surprise, although Gwayne hadn't missed the gesture which had clearly been made so the flashing diamonds and sapphires of Arleen's doubtlessly flawless rings didn't go unnoticed, but in her usual forthright manner Donna shrugged and gave an easy-going grin.

'As it's more than likely the only one I'll ever have, why wouldn't I keep it?' she countered.

Arleen smirked derisively. 'Goodness, what a shocking admission to have to make! But then all Brad's friends are like that, aren't they, Regan? They keep us amused the whole time they're here.'

But only maliciously, certainly never humorously, I bet, Gwayne fumed inwardly, her eyes clashing turbulently with silver-grey ones. No doubt he thought they were hilariously inferior too!

'How's the wrist?'

So absorbed had Gwayne been with her angry thoughts that it took a little time for his words to register, but when they did her head angled upwards challengingly.

'Quite good ... thank you,' she tacked on a trifle grudgingly.

'You didn't need to use it at all?'

Gwayne's lips twisted wryly. Not after the lengths she had been to in order to avoid doing just that! 'No,' she answered as nonchalantly as possible.

If he was satisfied with her answer, Donna was not, but sensing the other girl was about to relate the whole story, Gwayne quickly turned to Charlotte with an apologetic smile.

'I hope you'll excuse us, but we'd better keep going. We have to get cleaned up before dinner.'

'Of course, my dears, you go right ahead. I expect you're starving.'

'Just a little,' Donna agreed with feeling before they continued on their way, and to Gwayne immediately they were out of earshot, 'I gather you're staying in the shadows so they can't see your shirt sticking to your back, and the reason you jumped in so fast back there was because you knew I was going to mention it, wasn't it?' A short confirming nod and she peered at her companion closely. 'Now, would you mind telling me *why* you don't want them to know?'

'Because I feel self-conscious enough as it is,' Gwayne retorted. 'First I fall off a horse and injure my wrist, then I fall down the creek bank and hurt my back. Next, I'll probably fall out of bed and break a leg, or something equally ridiculous.' She gave a ruefully mocking smile. 'They'll think I'm a walking disaster area. That, or an irresponsible half-wit.'

'But it wasn't your fault you fell today,' Donna protested. 'I knocked you off balance.'

'The result's still the same,' Gwayne went to shrug, and thought better of it.

Donna didn't say any more on the subject until they had finally completed the painful task of removing Gwayne's shirt in the bath.

'They're bound to find out anyway,' she reasoned. 'Warren or Brad could say something, but even if they don't, someone's surely going to wonder why you're suddenly moving so carefully these days.'

'Oh, well, maybe in a day or two when it's on the mend it won't be so bad if they do all know.'

Donna dabbed tentatively at one particularly nasty gash with a piece of cotton wool. 'But I'm not sure they will all be on the mend in that short a time. There's a couple here I really don't like the look of, Gwayne,' she frowned worriedly. 'I wish we at least had some antiseptic to put on them.'

'Well, don't you dare ask Regan for any!' Gwayne swung her head round sharply, her expression fierce for a moment until her eyes started sparkling triumphantly. 'I know where there's some—the first aid kit in the Range Rover. We can use that.'

'That's a good idea,' Donna smiled with relief. 'You finish washing and I'll slip out and get it.'

'Make certain no one sees you.'

'Stop panicking, the Scarlet Pimpernel's got nothing on me,' Gwayne was informed with a grin, and then Donna was gone.

Without anything attached to her skin Gwayne was able to move a lot more freely and it didn't take long to wash and dry herself, except for her back which she left for Donna to attend to when she returned. With a large and fluffy buttercup yellow towel draped loosely about her she padded into the bedroom and gave her hair a good brush while she awaited her friend's reappearance. She didn't bother taking a nightdress from the drawer, having already decided she wouldn't be wearing one that night. She wasn't taking a chance on waking in the morning and finding something else firmly fastened to her, and figuring that if she slept on her stomach and left her back free for the air to reach, then maybe the cuts would have dried considerably by morning and she would be able to don a thin cotton shirt without fear of the same thing happening again.

A sound outside the door leading to the breezeway had her moving across the room as quickly as she was able and flinging it wide open. 'Did you manage to get it?' she burst out.

'Yes, I've got it, and now all I would like to know is why you want it?' drawled Regan as he came to stand in the doorway.

'Because I—because it's ...' Gwayne backed away from him nervously, her right hand clutching frantically at the towel, and all too embarrassedly aware of the skimpiness of her covering. 'I—why, I wanted a couple of aspirins, that's all,' she said the first thing that came into her head in desperation rather than inspiration. 'The trip home was rather bumpy and—and ...' She glanced apprehensively past him and queried breathlessly, 'Where's Donna?'

His mouth firmed uncompromisingly. 'I suggested she might care to have her dinner before she showered. Nora had it ready.'

'Oh, I see,' she smiled weakly, her gaze not quite connecting with his, and wishing she didn't feel so helplessly tired. So much for the Scarlet Pimpernell! 'Well, thank you for bringing it. I'm—I'm sorry to have taken you away from your guest.'

Instead of putting the kit down and leaving, as she had hoped he would, Regan paced further into the room and closed the door, much to Gwayne's dismay.

'You still haven't satisfactorily explained why you wanted it,' he prompted.

Yes, she had, hadn't she? Two creases made an appearance between her slim arching brows as she forced herself to remember. If only her brain wasn't as lethargic as the rest of her! Abruptly the thought returned.

'My headache,' she reminded him earnestly. 'I wanted some aspirin for it.'

'Strange!' Regan sent her a heavily sardonic glance which had her heart pounding jerkily against her ribs. 'Donna said you wanted some antiseptic for a cut on your leg.'

Involuntarily Gwayne looked down as his gaze ranged appraisingly over the shapely length of her limbs visible beneath the towel and her face flamed.

'No, no, she must have misunderstood me,' she prevaricated wildly. 'As you can see for yourself,' her colour flared higher, 'there are no cuts.'

'How about the backs of them?' He made a circling motion with one long forefinger. 'Turn around.'

'No!' It was a flat refusal as anger and indignation came to her aid. 'I'm damned if I'll be inspected like some slave on an auction block! Just who do you think you are, Regan? You've got no right coming in here and giving me orders!' she railed fierily.

'Don't you believe it, sweetheart,' he cautioned with such an assured smile that Gwayne would have struck him if she'd had a hand capable, or free, to do so. 'The minute you set foot on Fairfax Downs you were answerable to me for all your actions.'

A taunting look from the corner of her dark-fringed eyes and she gibed, 'Even to the taking of some aspirin? My, but you must have full days! I'm surprised you find the time to sleep.'

'Which I would probably do a whole lot easier if I didn't have to contend with an obstinate and defiant little redhead who seems insanely determined to ignore the fact that injuries require attention!'

'I was going to attend to it,' Gwayne hurled back heatedly. Hadn't Donna gone for the antiseptic? 'And I *will* attend to it if you'll kindly leave!' She went to turn her back on him dismissively, gave a horrified gasp of remembrance, and hurriedly faced him again. 'I'm— I'm waiting ...' she stammered an attempt at hauteur.

By way of a reply Regan tossed the first aid box carelessly on to the bed and strode towards her, his eyes glittering savagely. 'Then you're just going to have to damned well wait, you lying little ... !' he bit off an expletive furiously. 'There is a reason for your refusing to turn round, isn't there? But not the one you gave!' Catching hold of her arms, he roughly pulled her closer before Gwayne could back out of reach.

Until that moment she had never realised, nor even bothered to consider, how such an action stretched the muscles of the back, but now it felt as if her skin was being split into minute shreds and with a strangled cry she crumpled against his broad chest pleading, 'Oh, no, please don't!'

'Good God Almighty!' There was a moment's stunned silence and then, 'If you weren't that way already, I could beat you black and blue for trying to keep this a secret!' A hand beneath her chin forced pain-filled eyes up to his. 'In the name of heaven, Gwayne, *why*? Why this obsession with pretending you're not hurt when you are?' He let go of her chin and raked his hand through his hair with a heavy sigh. 'Is it a carry-over from your childhood, or is it just because of me?'

Still leaning against him—she doubted her legs would hold her if she moved away from his supporting strength—she shook her head weakly. Perhaps it was a little of both. At the home there had never been enough staff for them to have the time to pay too much attention to each child's hurts. More often than not it had merely been a case of a detached pat on the head together with the recommendation to 'be a brave little girl'. And Regan's presence? Well, she was finding that uncomfortably disturbing at any time, so it wasn't surprising that she was extremely wary of putting her emotions to the test when she was at her most defenceless.

'I don't know,' she shook her head again wearily. 'Maybe I'm just not a very confiding person.'

'Or fiercely independent ... because you've had to be?'

Gwayne gradually eased herself away from him and gave a faint smile. 'Now you're the one making excuses,' she charged shakily.

'And with you that could be a dangerous habit to acquire.'

She wasn't certain of his meaning, but his reaction was plain. He was annoyed. It was evident in the tightening of his well shaped lips and the stance of his lithely muscular frame as he collected the box from the bed. A hand indicated the padded stool in front of the dressing table and she was authoritatively ordered to, 'Sit!'

A command which had her glaring at him resentfully—she wasn't one of his sheepdogs!—but which she was too exhausted to dispute. She did, however, hitch her towel higher and protest, 'I would like to put on something a little more concealing, if you don't mind!'

Her complaint was squashed with an unconcerned, 'Don't worry, I know what the naked female body looks like.' Something it hadn't occurred to Gwayne to doubt! 'You probably wear a lot less when you go swimming.'

A good point, she was prepared to concede, although in this instance not necessarily a relevant one. Whenever she had been swimming she had never been this physically aware of anyone before!

She bit at her lip fretfully. 'But my hand aches from holding it. I can only use one.'

'Then pin it.' Regan dropped a large-sized safety-pin into her lap as he set the opened first aid case down on the dressing table.

But as Gwayne could only use one hand—and that hand was already importantly engaged—there wasn't much she could do with it. As he must have very well known! Wrathfully her breathing began to deepen and then, quite without warning and to her utter mortification, she started to cry.

In the next second Regan was on his haunches in front of her and fastening the pin with a minimum of fuss. 'There!' He gently unfurled the fingers which were still clinging to the towel and laid them in her lap, his lips taking on a remorseful curve. 'I'm sorry, sweetheart, you've had a rough day, haven't you?'

Blinking hard to halt the flow, and hastily wiping her fingers across her cheeks, Gwayne moved her head from side to side in disbelief. 'It was such a stupid little thing to cry about. I don't know what came over me. I'm not usually so weepy.'

'Just a case of the last straw and the camel's back, I'm thinking,' he smiled up at her so captivatingly that she felt suffocated. 'What you need is a good night's sleep. Let's get this antiseptic on, then you can have something to eat, and into bed,' as he gained his feet and picked up a bottle of yellow liquid.

'I couldn't eat a thing,' Gwayne sighed, her flesh shrinking away from his touch automatically, for although the antiseptic itself didn't sting, even the lightest of pressures on her skin was now painful. 'I've been looking forward to that bed for about the last four hours.'

'Brad shouldn't have kept you out there so long. Why

didn't he bring you home earlier when this happened?'

'Oh, he wanted to, a number of times,' she turned to assure him. 'But I wouldn't let him. It didn't feel so bad then.'

He worked on in silence for some minutes until he had intently surveyed one of the larger abrasions, whereupon he enquired thoughtfully, 'Are you up to date with your tetanus shots, Gwayne?'

She pulled a rueful face. 'I shouldn't think so. If I remember correctly I haven't had one since either just before or just after I started high school.' She swung her head to look at him with a frown. 'Why? Surely you're not suggesting there's a likelihood of my having picked that up?'

'There's always the possibility, and a couple of these cuts appear more inflamed than I would expect them to be.'

'But that doesn't mean it's tetanus!'

'I'm well aware of that, sweetheart, but you'll get a booster shot all the same,' was the peremptory retort. Followed by a just as forceful, 'I'll be going past Jeedara tomorrow, so you'd better come with me and we can call in at the hospital.'

'Do I have any choice?'

'Did you think I was giving you one?' mockingly.

'One can always hope,' she countered so dryly that he began to laugh.

Dressings were applied to those areas which needed them and Regan eyed his handiwork judiciously. 'Well, the colour may not be particularly attractive, but I think that's the best we can do for you at present,' he commented, screwing the cap back on the bottle and replacing it in the case. His fingers twined within her red-gold curls and tugged lightly. 'See if you can manage to get through the night without doing yourself any more harm, hmm?'

Nettled by the amusement in his voice, Gwayne sprang out of the chair and faced him smoulderingly. 'I don't do it on purpose, you know!' she flared. 'Others may be prepared to go to such lengths to gain the lordly Regan Fairfax's attention, but you can take my word for it that doesn't apply in my case!'

With his hands resting on lean hips, his eyes wandered lazily over her. 'Why should you?' he quizzed satirically. 'You appear to have far more successful methods of your own.'

'And just what's *that* supposed to mean?' she demanded.

Regan's mocking eyes did his talking for him and following their direction Gwayne let out a discomfited gasp. Her covering might have been wound tightly enough about her while she was sitting, but now she was on her feet it had descended to a gravity-defying level and she was unwittingly displaying almost every swelling curve she possessed.

'How dare you make such an insinuation?' she blazed, her cheeks burning as she furiously hauled the towel higher. 'I'll have you know I'm not—I wouldn't ... oh, why don't you go back to your girl-friend, Regan, and leave me alone? I'm sure she's a more rewarding proposition for you than I am, and she's probably well and truly missing your exhilarating company by now!'

He came round the chair towards her so purposefully that Gwayne took a swift step backwards, already regretting her impulsively reckless words, and swallowed nervously as he cupped her face firmly between his hands to query derisively,

'Who are you fighting, Gwayne? Me ... or yourself?'

The question was so totally unanticipated that she could only blink and stare at him confusedly, her mind a void, her emotions tumultuous. She knew without a shadow of a doubt what he was going to do next but was helpless to prevent it, and when his mouth lowered to hers she found herself accepting its dominance compliantly. It wasn't that she didn't want to resist, but Regan was no untried youth. He knew exactly what he was doing. His kisses aroused and tempted to such an extent that resistance was impossible—unthinkable—and Gwayne's lips clung to his unreservedly.

When he finally put her away from him it was to incline his head in a taunting salute. 'Now we know, don't we?' he mocked as he turned on his heel and made for the door.

Gwayne flushed to the roots of her hair as acquiescence was exchanged for humiliation. 'Why, you—you conceited beast!' she hurled after him, and wished it wasn't only words she was throwing. 'I hate you! I could never be attracted to someone like you!'

His only response was a finger raised to his forehead, his lips curving upwards tormentingly, and then she was left with only a closed door to vent her frustrations upon.

CHAPTER FIVE

BRAD wasn't very happy when he learnt at breakfast the following morning of Gwayne's intended trip with his cousin—in fact, he was furious—and immediately Regan left the table he had more than a few words to say about it.

'I notice he didn't bother to invite the rest of us to join you on this jaunt,' he gibed first.

Gwayne's smile was wry. 'I'd hardly call it a jaunt! The last tetanus shot I had left my arm feeling like a lump of lead.'

'It still doesn't take all day to have one lousy needle pushed into you. I'd just like to know what he's got planned for the rest of it.'

'Business, that's all,' she exclaimed. 'You heard him say that he had made arrangements for this trip days ago.'

'Sure, I heard him,' Brad agreed sarcastically. 'But that doesn't mean I have to believe him.'

Sherry brown eyes turned ceilingwards in despair. 'For heaven's sake, why would he lie?'

'To take you away from me would be reason enough for my cousin,' he retorted surlily.

'Oh, come on, old son,' Warren chipped in with a grin, and thereby earned Gwayne's gratitude. 'Aren't you getting a little carried away? We all know Gwayne would be better off with proper medical attention.'

Brad's eyes narrowed hostilely. 'Then why doesn't he call in the Flying Doctor?'

'Because he's going past a mission hospital himself.

I don't imagine these people waste valuable time calling the Flying Doctor Service unless it's absolutely imperative.'

A disgruntled snort and Brad proposed, 'In that case I should be the one to take her, not Regan!'

'But you haven't got a pilot's licence,' Warren laughed.

'So what? There's a road, isn't there?'

'If you're generous enough to call it that,' drily. 'Three hundred miles there and back wouldn't be my cup of tea, though. Hell, man, I thought the idea was to get your girl better, not make her worse.'

'Exactly my point!' Brad pounced smugly. 'Does he intend remembering that she's *my* girl?'

Gwayne thought it time she re-entered the conversation. 'Yes, well, when you've quite finished deciding who I belong to, Brad, I'd like to say a few words myself,' she cut in tartly. 'Just because I happen to be taking a plane trip with Regan it doesn't mean I'm about to become one of his devotees!' And especially not after last night.

'Huh! You don't know what he's like when he sets out to be charming ... I do! I've yet to see a female refuse him anything,' he retorted scornfully.

Donna clapped her hands together sharply. 'I believe it, I believe it!' she gurgled. 'Your cousin is one good-looking guy. Personable too,' she added roguishly.

'You see! She's only been here a day and a half and already she's singing his praises!'

'But I'm not, and I'm the one going with him,' Gwayne pointed out steadily.

'She's got you there, old son,' Warren grinned, and would have said more except that Charlotte Fairfax chose that moment to enter the dining room for her breakfast and Gwayne was very thankful when the subject was tactfully dropped.

The meal concluded, they all went their separate ways, Charlotte to have a word with Nora Wallace, Donna and Warren to make use of the tennis court, and Brad moodily accompanying Gwayne to her room as she collected her bag before meeting Regan at the garage.

From the chair he watched her reflection in the mirror as she ran a comb through her hair and renewed her lipstick. 'You think I'm being childish over this, don't you?' he frowned.

'A little,' she owned truthfully. 'If I hadn't had that fall yesterday I wouldn't have needed to go with him, but I'm sure the thought of annoying you wasn't the reason he suggested it.'

Brad chewed this over carefully. 'But are you positive you have to go at all? It is a lot better this morning, isn't it?'

'Except for a couple of places,' she agreed. 'Although in one sense I'm the wrong person to ask. I'm the only one who can't have a good look at them. Donna did, though, while I was getting dressed and said she thought it would be advisable.'

He swung to his feet and came to stand behind her, his arms encircling her slim figure, his chin resting on the top of her head. 'Just try not to be away too long, hmm? I shall be eaten up with jealousy the whole time you're gone,' he let out his breath heavily.

'There's no need to be,' Gwayne smiled up at him persuasively as she turned within his arms and linked her own about his waist. 'I'm not interested in chasing after Regan, and as he already has a girl-friend who seems eminently suited to the master of Fairfax Downs,

I can't honestly see him paying any undue attention to a little nobody like me. I don't have the right
background and connections, you know,' she grinned
teasingly.

'But you do have a beautiful face and an enticing
shape. A month's fling to spite me could be a tempting
proposition for him.'

One winged brow rose ironically. 'Thanks for the
vote of confidence, but I'll have you know it's not a
habit of mine to indulge in casual flings!'

'And who should know that better than I? I'm sorry,
honey,' he apologised sincerely, looking abashed. 'Maybe I am making mountains out of molehills.'

'Besides which, you're forgetting I've never been in
a plane before.' It was Gwayne's turn to look rueful
now. 'It's quite possible I shall feel as sick as a dog ...
and a nauseous, bandaged,' she lifted her wrist into his
line of vision, 'lacerated, sore-armed booster-reacting
female wouldn't be my ideal for a romantic companion,' she laughed.

'I suppose you're right,' he allowed with a grudging
wryness. 'As long as ...'

'Brad! Stop worrying about things you can't be certain will happen!'

'Okay, okay.' His lips met hers in a long possessive
kiss which left Gwayne feeling strangely unaffected.
'I'll join the others at the courts and see if I can keep
my mind busy that way.'

Gwayne merely nodded. If she said anything it would
surely start him off again. A glance at her watch
showed the time for their departure to be close and
she hastily bundled a few necessary items into a leather
bag and slipped sunglasses on to her nose. With Brad's
hand gently resting on her waist they left the room
together.

Relieved that he didn't accompany her all the way to the garage but said goodbye with Donna and Warren —thus precluding any confrontation with Regan from taking place—Gwayne didn't speak on the ride out to the airstrip. She was nervous about taking her first flight but was determined to conceal her apprehension as much as possible and concentrated on the scenery as they sped away from the compound.

Neither did Regan speak until they were airborne——an eventuality Gwayne had never thought would come to pass when they were thundering towards the trees at the end of the strip, but finally the nose had lifted gracefully and the green barrier had disappeared below them.

'Don't you like flying?' were his first enquiring words, which she answered with a light shrug and a deprecating,

'I wouldn't know really. This is the first time I've done any.'

White teeth gleamed in an understanding smile. 'You should have said something.'

'Would it have made any difference?'

'First take-offs and landings normally bring out a few butterflies. I could have explained what I was doing. It helps settle the nerves if you know what's going on.'

'What makes you think I'm nervous?'

'Most of my passengers don't sit there trying to squeeze the life out of their fingers,' she was informed dryly. 'Nor do they give a choked gasp and close their eyes when we're about to leave the ground.'

Gwayne rapidly untwined her fingers with an excusing, 'Well, those trees, they were ...' She broke off to reprove indignantly, 'Wouldn't it be safer if you kept your eyes on the controls instead of on me?'

He slanted her a fathomless glance and then the one corner of his mouth that she could see tilted humorously. 'Do I detect some of Brad's coaching's in that statement?'

'I don't know what you're getting at,' she shrugged away the question haughtily.

'You mean, he willingly let you come with me? He didn't credit me with some sly traitorous reason for having suggested it?' he taunted incredulously.

His assumption was so accurate that there was no way Gwayne could deny it. Her only chance at retaliation was to launch a counter-attack, which she did with a sarcastic look from beneath curling lashes.

'You enjoy making fun of him all the time, don't you?' she censured.

'Far from it,' Regan denied with a decisive movement of his head. 'In actual fact I feel sorry for him. Brad's trouble borders on being a sickness.' A tanned hand ensnared her chin. 'It's been something of a revelation for you, hasn't it, Gwayne?' he probed, seriously for once.

'I—I'm ...' She couldn't hold that crystal clear gaze any longer and her eyelids fluttered down defensively. 'You could take it easier on him if you wanted to,' she reproached.

'For all the good it would do. There's only one thing Brad wants from me.'

'Fairfax Downs,' Gwayne sighed, her expression troubled.

'So you found out after all. Did he tell you, or did you guess?'

'No, he told me.' She half turned towards him impulsively, temporarily forgetting the antagonism she had been harbouring since their last meeting. 'He really believes it should all be his, Regan. He's so different from how he normally is in Sydney that I find it hard to believe. It's almost as if I don't know him any more.'

'Well, there's no need for you to worry yourself over it, sweetheart,' he gave her a calmly reassuring smile. 'Provided he continues to reserve his bitterness for me not much harm can come of it.'

'Doesn't it worry you?'

'Let's just say I've become used to it after all these years,' he drawled. 'In my presence at least it just wouldn't be Brad if he didn't make one resentful remark.'

'Just as it wouldn't be you if you didn't make a goading one?' she had to challenge.

His dark brows quirked expressively. 'Are we still talking about Brad, or have you now reduced the conversation to a more personal level?'

Gwayne pressed her lips together and swung her gaze away vexedly. She didn't need to be very bright to know he was referring to that remark he had addressed to her last night. A few strongly disciplining breaths and she was able to retort coolly,

'No, I haven't, but thank you for proving my point all the same. You're an infuriating devil, Regan!'

'Overtones of Brad again?' he immediately quizzed uncontritely, and had her glowering at him resentfully.

'Oh, you're impossible! Completely and utterly impossible!' she flared.

His ensuing laughter didn't make her feel any better and she stared out of the window unseeingly, her breasts heaving. How could she let herself be attracted to someone who was so deliberately and damnably aggravating? Why couldn't she just ignore his baiting remarks and him along with them? She would be far less vulnerable if she did.

Jeedara township was typical of many such places in

the outback with its wide and dusty main street, its small complement of awning-shaded buildings, and its air of remoteness as it lay still and quiet beneath the scorching sun. A tiny oasis of habitation in the midst of the isolated inland. But Jeedara was more favoured than most—it had a mission hospital, a low building constructed of local stone and surrounded by its own neatly kept gardens, and which served as the medical and dental centre for outlying districts covering some thousands of square miles.

Passing through the gauze front door, Regan led Gwayne along a wide corridor where fan-induced breezes provided some relief from the soaring temperature. Halfway down there was an unoccupied bench outside an open door which showed into a large and, to Gwayne's eyes, surprisingly well equipped surgery.

At their entrance the middle-aged man who had been sitting at the table facing the doorway rose quickly to his feet and came towards them exclaiming pleasurably,

'Regan, it's good to see you! What brings you out this way? A social call and not a professional one, I trust,' as they shook hands firmly.

'A little of both, John,' Regan smiled in explanation. 'I had some business with Simon anyway, so when Gwayne,' he broke off to make the introduction, 'Gwayne Peters, meet John Foster, our local medico,' and once the appropriate acknowledgments had been made, continued, 'so when Gwayne had a fall while out prospecting yesterday we thought it best to combine the two.'

We thought it best! Gwayne sent him an ironic glance from the corner of her eye but forbore to correct him. Now was not the time for remonstrations.

John's rounded face broke into a cherubic smile. 'Well, it can't be too serious, you're still on your feet.

A large percentage of my patients aren't.' He ushered her towards the seat in front of the table and then with a glance at the clock on the wall turned to Regan. 'I expect Jane and Betty will be putting the kettle on about now, so you might like to join them. They'll be pleased to see you after so long too. I'll have mine in here,' he advised, and over his shoulder, 'What about you, Gwayne? Would you like some tea?'

A heartfelt, 'Yes, please,' and Regan closed the door as he left. No doubt to make the day for the unknown Jane and Betty, decided Gwayne with such unaccustomed asperity that it shocked her.

When John escorted her out of the surgery some thirty minutes later Regan was already waiting for them, a half-smoked cigarette between his fingers.

'Okay?' His gaze was directed at the doctor rather than Gwayne.

'Okay,' came the encouraging confirmation. 'There may be a sore arm for a few hours, and there was a slight infection for which I've prescribed some antibiotics, but otherwise all sound and healthy.'

He walked to the verandah with them, his kindly brown eyes twinkling as he said to Gwayne, 'Let's hope the rest of your holiday isn't quite so eventful, and that our next meeting is purely a social one.' And following it with a brow-raised enquiry to Regan, 'You will be going to the Halfords' gymkhana, I take it?'

'Yes, we'll be well represented. Les is anxious to avenge his defeat of last year and there's plenty willing to bet that he does,' wryly. 'As for Gwayne and the others ...' He shrugged offhandedly. 'Well, the choice is up to them.'

It sounded as if he didn't expect them to attend and Gwayne stared at him doubtfully. 'Are we invited?' she asked of them generally.

'No invitations issued, none needed,' John took it upon himself to reply. 'It's just a good opportunity for everyone to get together and enjoy themselves, and raise some money for charity at the same time.'

'I see.' She chewed at her bottom lip thoughtfully. 'How—how would we get there?'

'We usually drive when it's held on Copeland,' Regan was the one to inform her this time, while John urged, 'You come, Gwayne, you'll be made very welcome. A new face is always eagerly greeted out here.'

'And especially by all the single men if it happens to be an extremely pretty one,' inserted Regan dryly.

The older man chuckled pleasantly. 'More than a possibility, I grant you, but come anyway, Gwayne, won't you?'

'I'll have a word with the others about it,' she smiled as they prepared to take their leave. 'And thank you for the treatment. I'll try not to need your services again while I'm here.'

'That's the girl,' he approved warmly, lifting a hand in farewell. 'I'll see you at the gymkhana, Regan.'

'Right, John—and thanks!'

'My pleasure.'

The airstrip was hardly more than a hundred yards from the rear of the hospital, so it was only a short walk back to the plane and in a matter of minutes they were again nosing up into the cloudless sky, but without Gwayne showing any nervousness this time as Regan helpfully explained what he was doing, why, and what action would result because of it.

As soon as they had levelled off Gwayne enquired hesitantly, 'What do they do at the gymkhana?'

'A little bit of everything. If your imagination stretches that far, I guess you could best describe it as something of a cross between the picnic races, a bushman's carnival, and a fête,' he grinned.

'It sounds fun,' said Gwayne, her expression faintly wistful.

'They usually are,' he agreed.

'But you don't expect us to go, do you?'

Wide shoulders lifted indolently. 'What makes you say that?'

'The way you spoke back there when John first mentioned it.'

'I said it was your decision, that's all. I could hardly presume to make the choice for you.'

'You would if you felt like it, I'm sure,' she countered acidly, temporarily diverted.

'And you want me to, is that it?' His brows flicked upwards in mock-astonishment.

'No, that isn't it!' she disclaimed angrily. 'I'm perfectly capable of making my own decisions without any help from you.'

'Then there's nothing to stop you from going to Copeland if you wish, is there?'

In some indefinable way Gwayne felt the whole nature of their conversation had suddenly been reversed and that she was now the one being put on the spot instead of vice versa. Accordingly, her response was warily given.

'I—well, I suppose not really,' she stammered. 'Providing the others want to go as well, of course.'

'And if they don't?' His eyes were openly taunting. 'Do you need their permission, or are you just too timid to go without them?'

'No, to both questions!' Gwayne retaliated impatiently. 'It's just that—it's ...'

'So where's the problem?' he interposed smoothly. 'You did say the decision was *yours* to make, and you do want to go, don't you?'

'Yes—yes, I do, but—but I ...'

Her voice trailed away uncertainly and a crease channelled its way across her forehead. She had that feeling of having been stampeded again, of him having made the decision even though it had been herself who announced it. She settled back in her seat and cast him a deeply suspicious sideways glance. She might not know what game Regan was playing, but one thing she was certain about. He wasn't going to have it all his own way if she could help it!

For the remainder of the flight, to Gwayne's relief, their conversation involved less worrying topics as they passed over vast tracts of tree-studded plains where great herds of kangaroos could be seen basking in the sunlight, and flocks of sulphur-crested cockatoos adorned branches like plump white and yellow Christmas decorations. Her back was less bothersome now that it had been re-dressed at the hospital, her arm only slightly sore from the injection, and she was finding she thoroughly enjoyed flying—without feeling the least bit queasy—and especially at an altitude where it was possible to see so much happening on the ground. As a mode of transport she was totally in favour of it.

It was approaching lunchtime when they began their descent at Murramai. A downward path which gave Gwayne plenty of time to look over the square shaped homestead and note quite a number of differences in the layout from that used on Regan's property.

'His yards are much higher and heavier than yours ... why's that?' she queried interestedly.

Intent on landing, Regan didn't answer until they were safely down and slowing. 'Because Simon grazes cattle in the main, not sheep,' he enlightened her equably. 'That's the reason for this trip. To buy another bull.'

'But if you run sheep what do you want with a bull?'
she frowned.

He brought the plane round at the end of the strip
and began taxiing back. 'There are cattle on Fairfax
Downs too,' he laughed at her puzzled expression.
'Someone has to provide meat for all those people on
the property, a general diet of lamb and chicken can become very monotonous.' His dusky-framed eyes gleamed
banteringly. 'Where did you think it all came from ...
the local corner butcher?'

Not likely when the nearest was goodness knows how
many miles away! She hunched one shoulder self-
consciously and confessed, 'I never thought about it, I
guess.' And in an effort to distract his attention from
her ignorance, 'How—how many cattle do you have?'

'Not many—about three hundred in all.'

Gwayne wasn't prepared to dispute his statement—
they were obviously judging by different sets of values—
and bent instead to unbuckle her seat-belt as they
rolled to a halt.

A vehicle with a stockman relegated to driver was
waiting alongside the strip and it was a relatively swift
ride across the paddock to the wisteria-festooned house.
Pausing for a moment to inhale the fragrance being
emitted by the foot-long mauve blooms, Gwayne didn't
at first see the tall, greying-haired man who came out
on to the verandah to greet them, but on hearing
Regan warmly acknowledging another presence she
hurried up the steps behind him. Simon Houghton—
for she presumed it was he—would have been in his
late fifties by Gwayne's reckoning, a pleasant-faced,
spare-framed man with somewhat sad hazel eyes whose
pleased countenance underwent an alarming change
when she stepped into view.

'Oh, my God, it's Judy!' he gasped in a strangled

tone, his face whitening beneath his tan to an unbelievable degree.

Gwayne's immediate reaction was to take a quick step forward thinking he might be ill, but on seeing a discerning perception beginning to spread over Regan's features she came to a standstill and stared perplexedly from one to the other.

'Of course! Judy Ashcroft!' Regan softly broke the silence which had fallen after his friend's stunned exclamation. 'I told you I knew your face from somewhere. You're a dead ringer for her,' he asserted with calm insistence.

Still on edge after the older man's anguished reception, Gwayne inexplicably found herself challenging, 'Considering you couldn't remember two days ago, you're suddenly remarkably confident, aren't you?'

'But he's right, child,' Simon corroborated quietly, his colour assuming a more natural hue, and held an arm outstretched towards the doorway. 'If you would care to come inside I can give you positive proof.'

'That I happen to look like someone else?' she queried uneasily without making any attempt to accept his invitation.

'What's wrong, Gwayne?' Regan lowered his head fractionally closer to goad, 'Surely you're not ...'

'What name did you say?' he was interrupted sharply.

Straightening, Regan smiled apologetically. 'I'm sorry, I didn't introduce you, did I?' And after having performed this duty, he added, 'Gwayne came up with Brad and two other friends for a month's holiday.'

'That's nice,' Simon nodded, then cleared his throat and fixed Gwayne with an intent gaze. 'Tell me, is yours a popular name in the city these days?' he asked interestedly. 'I'm afraid I'm a little out of touch with the current fads and fancies in that direction.'

It was much the same comment as Regan had originally made, and that Simon should now have done the same thing unaccountably made her as nervous as a kitten.

'No, it's not one that's on everybody's lips,' she tried to laugh away her feelings of disquiet, but only succeeded in sounding shaky. 'In fact, I've never heard of anyone else called the same.'

'It just held some significance for your parents, eh?'

If it hadn't been for Regan's hand at her waist relentlessly urging her down the hallway into the attractively furnished lounge, she would have come to a complete halt again. As it was her spine stiffened apprehensively. Just what was Simon Houghton trying to prove?

'Gwayne never knew her parents. She was brought up in a children's home,' Regan answered for her, and was presented with a fierce glare for his efforts. What right did he have to pass on details of her personal history?

As they took their seats on a chintz-covered couch Regan's eyes followed their host speculatively as he made for the lacquered bamboo bar. 'Any particular reason for asking, Simon?' he probed, to Gwayne's vexation.

Before replying Simon sounded their preferences— sherry for Gwayne, beer for Regan—poured and handed them their appropriate glasses, then took a matching armchair opposite.

'I had a young sister who died of polio when she was only twelve,' he began slowly, seemingly absorbed in watching the bubbles rise within his own glass. 'Her name was Gwayne too.'

'I—I'm sorry, but that's quite a coincidence, isn't it?'

Gwayne made certain she spoke for herself this time, her tone falsely light.

'I'm beginning to wonder,' countered Simon as his gaze came up to hers with a crooked semblance of a smile.

'Oh?' Gwayne deliberately forced herself to take a sip of her drink to relieve her tension. 'What makes you say that?'

In lieu of a reply he rose to his feet, took a framed photograph from the roll-top desk which stood against one wall, and held it out to her. Having taken it with nerveless fingers, it was some time before Gwayne could bring herself to look at it, but when she did her breath caught in her throat.

It was for all the world as if she was looking into a mirror. Except for a slightly shorter length of hair the girl was her exact double, even down to her even white teeth. It was uncanny. She raised widened eyes to find both men surveying her closely and swallowed hard.

'Judy Ashcroft?' she surmised faintly.

Simon nodded, and from the expression on his face Gwayne knew without question that he must have loved the laughing girl in the picture very much, but a finger under her chin turned her face towards him as Regan drawled, 'What price coincidence now?' had her thoughts returning to her own problems and jumping away from him as if stung.

'But that's all it is!' she declared positively. 'You can't really believe there's some connection between us!'

'Of course there has to be a connection, you're far too much alike for it to be otherwise,' he retorted inflexibly.

'That's still no reason to ...' She stopped in order to put forward another point in her argument. 'But I was born in Sydney—nowhere near here!'

'Then how about this for another piece of coincidence?' he proposed ironically. 'Judy moved to Sydney a year before she was killed.'

The consequences of what he was implying were overwhelming and Gwayne just couldn't bring herself to accept them—it was all happening too fast and too unexpectedly—and within seconds of putting her glass on the low table in front of them she was on her feet and staring down at him resentfully.

'Which all proves ... *nothing!*' she stormed. 'I don't care if I do look like her,' stabbing a finger towards the photograph lying beside him on the couch. 'I'm not interested in listening to you trying to justify some inconclusive theory just because of a facial resemblance and a couple of unverifiable facts which happen to have coincided. Now, why don't you just conduct the business which occasioned this visit and leave me alone!'

She swung to face Simon with an embarrassed look. 'I'm sorry, I don't usually walk into someone else's home and promptly blow my top, but ...' She spread her hands wide in a helpless gesture. 'If you don't mind, I think I'd better take a walk outside and cool off,' as she marched out of the room, her head held at a defiant angle.

On the verandah Gwayne drew a hurried breath, as if to dispel the disquieting suggestions which had been created, and hastened down the steps into the garden. She had no particular direction in mind to follow and let her feet lead her aimlessly where they willed, past the stores shed and workshop where she acknowledged easy-going greetings from a couple of Simon's employees, and on to the horse yards. A brown stock horse, reminding her of Puppet, caught her attention as he stood within the shade of a giant pepper tree and leaning over the top rail of the fence she called to him persuasively. Ears pricked, he turned to look at her inquisitively and then obediently trotted across the yard so she could pat his satin-smooth neck and stroke his velvety nose.

A while later, from the corner of her eye, she noticed Regan and Simon disappear inside one of the out-buildings set behind the yards, but made no move to join them. Although she would have been interested to hear their discussion regarding the bull Regan was intending to purchase and see the animal for herself— which was doubtless what they were doing now—for the time being she preferred the peaceful uncomplica-ted company of her four-legged friend. Presently they reappeared together with a third man, and began walk-ing along the path which led back to the house, their discourse still continuing.

A roan ambled up to share her attentions and tem-porarily she was diverted from the men's progress, and it wasn't until a voice sounded beside her that she realised Simon had returned on his own.

'Do you like horses?' he questioned affably, leaning on the rail next to her, and on noting her slight hesi-tation added with a half laugh, 'Don't worry, I won't say, "So did Judy", if you agree.'

Surprised by his shrewd insight, Gwayne dipped her head shyly in acquiescence. 'Yes, I do like them,' she admitted, and even offered, 'I suppose like a lot of people who missed out on having a pet of their own as children, animals have always held a certain fascina-tion for me.'

'Ever done any riding?'

'Only once, and then I did this,' she indicated her

bandaged wrist ruefully. 'But I'm still eager to have another try. It's something I've always wished I could do.'

He smiled at her enthusiasm and then his face sobered. 'I know you took exception to our questioning earlier, and I apologise, but if I told you a little more about the events which instigated it, perhaps it would explain my reasons and help you to understand. May I?' he appealed quietly, anxiously.

It would be churlish to refuse, Gwayne decided. He was only asking her to heed ... not to concede. 'All right,' she nodded.

Simon scanned the faded blue sky wryly. 'Well, it's too hot for you out here without a hat. How about we make use of that tree over there?' singling out a bauhinia close by. 'Or maybe you would prefer the verandah?' His brows lifted enquiringly.

'No, the tree will be fine,' Gwayne smiled, and gave each horse one last pat before they moved away. 'I like it out here. It's so clean and clear and exhilarating you feel there's nothing you couldn't do if you really put your mind to it.' She half laughed self-consciously, her shoulders hunching. 'That's one of its secret weapons for devastating the unprepared, I suppose.'

'Oh, it can take you in all right, and especially during a good season like this one,' he endorsed knowledgeably. 'But if your heart's big enough, your back's strong enough, and you keep your feet well and truly planted on the ground, you can usually manage to make a go of it. Most of us who have made the outback our home wouldn't choose to live anywhere else.'

Gwayne could understand that. To be able to overcome such excessive and ruthless challenges as this land threw out would be extremely satisfying as well as rewarding.

'Would you care for a cigarette?' Simon asked as they eased themselves comfortably up on to the boards of an old dray someone was evidently in the process of refurbishing.

'Please!' gratefully. She somehow sensed she might have need of it.

'Well ...' he sighed, and flicked her an abstracted smile, his thoughts already returning to the past, 'I've lived on this property just about all my life—my father having bought it when I was a lad of six—and it's become an essential part of that life. I didn't marry until after I'd turned thirty and then, unluckily, to a girl who had been raised in the city and who imagined living in the outback was going to be a romantic adventure.'

He paused and drew heavily on his cigarette before continuing. 'Unfortunately for Vera it didn't work out that way. It was a lot tougher out here in those days. Oh, it was better than it had been, we had the Flying Doctor and the pedal radio, but no telephones or small aircraft which have done so much to cut down that feeling of complete isolation. To travel from here to Fairfax Downs wasn't a matter of a few hours' comfortable flying, it took a couple of days by car over some of the worst tracks you can imagine. Anyway, we'd only been married for six months when Vera decided it wasn't for her and began badgering me to sell up and go elsewhere to live—the city for preference.' His eyes turned wryly skywards.

'Naturally, I didn't want to—apart from the fact that I wasn't trained for any other work, I liked the life—and one afternoon we had a tremendous argument about it which resulted in her tearing off on a half broken stallion we'd only had in the yards for a couple of weeks but which she'd been determined to ride. They'd only gone two hundred yards before he threw her and broke her back—a fall which left her a bedridden invalid for the rest of her life,' he recalled strickenly.

A shiver of sensory compassion trickled down Gwayne's spine at the picture he painted, but she judged it not the time to interrupt and sensitively waited for him to take up the narration.

'She never returned here after she left hospital, but went straight to Sydney,' he sighed. 'Half a dozen times I went down there to try and persuade her to come back, but she wasn't interested. She blamed me for the accident—I do myself—and as far as she was concerned everything was washed up between us. The only thing left for me to do was to see she never wanted for anything, which I did willingly.'

A sharp exhalation and he shook his head to dismiss the painful memories. 'Two years later the Ashcrofts took over the hotel in Jeedara and in time young Judy and I fell in love. Maybe I should have stayed away from town, I don't know, but it created an impossible situation,' he ran a hand wretchedly around his neck. 'I was married with no chance of a divorce. I couldn't possibly have asked Vera for one after what happened, and I very much doubt she would have agreed anyway. On top of that, at thirty-six, I was twice Judy's age! Her parents were strongly opposed to our friendship, and how could I blame them? I didn't think our association fair to her either. Judy said she didn't care whether we were married or not, as long as we could be together, and one Saturday when I drove in to town to see her, she was waiting for me at the end of the street, her packed bags alongside her. Apparently her parents had tried to forbid her from seeing me again.'

'So what did you do?' Gwayne whispered throatily.

'I did the most ill-judged thing I could possibly have

done,' he related remorsefully. 'I brought her back to Murramai with me. Oh, I was full of good intentions, of course, but I was also old enough to have known better. I loved that girl more than I thought it was possible to love anyone, and I don't think I need explain to you what occurred between us that night, do I?'

An understanding shake of Gwayne's head and he went on, 'In the morning the problem was understandably worse, not better. I was now faced with one of two choices. Did I keep her with me and flaunt our unmarried state before the community at large—and remember, *de facto* wives were not so common nor so readily accepted in those days—or did I do what I should have done the night before and take her back to her parents for the sake of her reputation?'

It was obvious he was finding it distressing, so Gwayne thought to help by prompting, 'And you did the latter?'

'I thought it was in her best interests,' he groaned.

'Then what happened?' she asked as calmly as possible.

'For a while things continued much as before, only the strain was worse now on both of us, so after about two months I suggested it might be better if we didn't see each other quite so often. As much as the idea hurt, I kept thinking that if I gave her a chance, and with her being so young, her affections might change and she would be able to look forward to a future with someone who could offer her marriage.'

From what she had heard so far Gwayne didn't think that at all likely, but she had to ask, 'And did she?' all the same.

Simon shook his head slowly. 'No, but a few weeks later she suddenly left Jeedara for Sydney without even letting me know she was going,' he grieved. 'She wrote a few times—stilted, unnatural little notes which didn't sound like her at all—but never marked with a return address and always posted from the General Post Office so there was no hope of tracing her.'

He put out his cigarette and rubbed the tips of his fingers across his forehead. 'A year after that I received word that Vera had died. Always a big eater, she'd steadily become more and more overweight since the accident until her heart could stand the strain no longer and had finally given out.'

A pause to control his ragged breathing and, 'When I arrived home from the funeral I was advised that during my visit to Sydney the police had notified Duncan and Carrie Ashcroft that Judy had been killed in a car smash on the highway only a hundred miles east of Jeedara. According to the sole survivor of the accident, the driver of the car she was travelling in, she'd said she was hitch-hiking home because she was short of money, but if everything went as she hoped she would have something very special to show everyone when she returned from her next trip.'

During the silence that followed Gwayne swallowed jerkily and avoided his waiting gaze. 'I—I'm sorry it couldn't have turned out happier for you, but th-thank you for telling me,' she half smiled in commiseration as she slid off the dray and nervously ground out her cigarette. Then, for want of something better to say, 'Does—does Regan know the whole story?'

'Yes, he's always known most of it, of course. He was about twelve or thirteen when Judy left. I filled him in on the rest after you left us.'

'I see.' She ran her hands down the sides of her slacks and moved restively from one foot to the other. 'I—um—suppose it's only to be expected that everyone knows everyone else's business in such a small community.'

'Mmm, although that can be an advantage at times,' he replied a little vaguely, his thoughts obviously moving along other lines, and their direction unfortunately becoming all too clear when he questioned, 'How old are you, Gwayne?'

A temptation to add or subtract a year assailed her, but she eventually ignored it. 'Twenty-one.'

'And how did you come to be placed in the orphanage? Did something happen to your parents?'

'Not that I know of,' she returned stiffly. 'They just didn't want me.'

Simon seemed disappointed and Gwayne was able to sigh with relief. But not for long, because a mocking voice was only too ready to prompt, 'You forgot to tell him about the note.'

'What note?' Simon demanded, but Gwayne was too incensed to pay him any attention and whirled around to snap at her tormentor,

'Why can't you just for once mind your own damned business, Regan? This has nothing whatsoever to do with you!'

'But you do admit it *does* have something to do with *you*!'

'Not in the way you're trying to imply,' she denied.

His grey eyes narrowed subtly. 'And just what way's that?'

'By implying that she—that I ...' A determined brake was put on her words and her chin slanted upwards mutinously. 'Well, you're wrong! The idea's just too fanciful for words!' she retorted with a deliberately provoking sarcasm.

'Only because you're too damned obstinate to recognise the possibility when it's staring you in the face!'

he retaliated scathingly. 'It's about time someone ...'

'Hold it, hold it!' came the amused call to order from Simon as he put up a restraining hand. 'Do you two always fight like this?'

'Yes!' flashed Gwayne immediately, but Regan's answer was slower in coming. His mouth tilted lazily as he drawled, 'No, not always,' with such unmistakable meaning that fiery flames of colour suffused Gwayne's cheeks and she was forced to drop her gaze in embarrassment.

Simon's hand swept gently over her bright hair, his kindly face tolerant as he smiled down at her. 'I think with this one, the more you push the more opposition you'll find,' he remarked wryly to Regan. And to Gwayne, 'As it's time for lunch, suppose we adjourn to the house, hmm? I suspect this morning has been as disconcerting for you as it has been for me.'

A conjecture Gwayne had no intention of opposing!

CHAPTER SIX

THROUGHOUT their appetising meal in the elegantly appointed Victorian dining room Gwayne was aware of Simon tactfully avoiding any reference of a personal nature, and as the meal progressed knew her resolute stand to be under siege from within. Was she really being fair in refusing him information which he clearly believed to be of significance, even if she didn't? If she was right, it would prove once and for all there was no connection between Judy Ashcroft and herself except that, extraordinarily, they had been born with identical features. But if she was wrong ...? She shook the thought away confidently. How could she be? It was just too fantastic to contemplate!

Glancing up, she found Regan's smoky gaze examining her meditatively across the table, a disturbing assessment which had her pulse faltering and her emotions reeling. Desperate to resist his dangerous attraction, she swung to face Simon, the question she had been parrying all morning being spoken without any conscious volition.

'You think I'm Judy Ashcroft's daughter, don't you?' she sighed.

If ever there had been a significant silence they were experiencing one now. There was absolute quiet in those first few seconds—but which seemed like minutes —after her words had tumbled from her lips. Regan's reaction was, in Gwayne's view, surprising—merely sitting back in his chair, his expression unreadable as he waited patiently for events to take their course.

Simon's was more predictable. His eyes shone with relief and ... gratitude? When he spoke his voice was low and careful.

'More to the point perhaps at the moment is the fact that I believe it's quite possible you could be *my* daughter,' he said.

'Oh!' Strangely enough that wasn't an eventuality she had considered.

'I'm sorry if I've shocked you,' he leant across and patted her arm sympathetically. 'Is the idea so upsetting?'

'Upsetting?' she repeated dazedly, and combed her hair back from her temples with unsteady fingers. 'No —no, not upsetting exactly. It's just that—that there's no proof for any of it.'

'But I believe there's a considerable amount of proof to justify such an assumption,' Simon contradicted softly. 'Unsubstantiated at present maybe, but not impossible to verify now that we know of your existence, I'm sure.'

That frightening feeling of being swamped by circumstances was attacking her again and Gwayne hurried to put an obstacle in its path. 'But how can you?' she questioned. 'They never even knew who left me at the home.'

'Mmm, that could perhaps make things difficult, although ...' He stopped with a frown and eyed her closely. 'When I asked you outside if anything had happened to your parents, you said something to the effect that they hadn't wanted you. How would you have known that?'

She shrugged with convincing ignorance. 'Well, why else would they have ...'

'Gwayne!' The long drawling admonishment had her biting at her lip guiltily and refusing to meet

Regan's sardonic glance. 'You seem to have forgotten that note again,' he taunted.

Now she did return his regard—wrathfully. 'Knowing you're here for the sole purpose of reminding me, how could I possibly?' she sniped.

'Ah, yes, I'd forgotten that myself,' Simon put in swiftly before Regan had an opportunity to reply. 'What did it say exactly?'

With one last resentful glare across the table, Gwayne recounted tautly, 'It just told them my name and said they would return for me, that's all.'

'I see,' he mused speculatively. 'And when was this, do you know?'

'Some time in March, I was told. I don't know the exact day.'

Simon's gaze met Regan's expressively and, seeing it, Gwayne decried mockingly, 'Now I suppose you're going to tell me that was the month Judy Ashcroft left Sydney.'

'Only because it's the truth,' Simon insisted. 'She died on the eleventh.'

'That still doesn't prove anything,' she denied with a vigorous shake of her head. 'None of it does. It's all only speculation.'

'But extremely plausible speculation, I'm sure you would agree.' A thoughtful frown and he enquired, 'Haven't you ever wanted to know who your parents were, Gwayne?'

'Not particularly,' she shrugged. 'If they didn't want me then there wasn't much point in knowing who they were, was there?'

'Not quite what I was meaning, I'm afraid. Perhaps I didn't word it as well as I could have done,' he smiled ruefully. 'I was attempting to ask if you'd never experienced a wish to share your life with your parents?'

That was an entirely different question and Gwayne's thoughts involuntarily flashed back over the years. Oh, yes, she'd wanted that! Hadn't every child in the home? But as she had grown older she had learnt to suppress any of those distressing types of feelings.

'When I was younger I did,' she finally divulged, her eyes focusing upon her fingers as they methodically twisted her wine glass around on the tablecloth. 'But by the time I left the home I guess I'd become reconciled to the fact that I didn't have a family, and now ...' Her shoulders lifted helplessly and she flicked him a regretful glance. 'Well, I don't really know if I— if I ...'

'Want one?' he concluded sadly.

'Oh, no, that wasn't what I was trying to say,' she rejected his supposition immediately. 'It's just that after having been completely independent for so long I don't know if I could fit in,' wryly.

'But you would be willing to try?' he pressed.

Gwayne took a mental step backwards, unconsciously resisting. 'I couldn't really say until I was actually faced with the situation.'

'All right, I can understand that,' he conceded, and then his eyes shone with a disarming twinkle. 'But I'll keep you to it when it turns out I'm correct.'

'*If*,' she insisted indomitably, but with a responding smile as she felt herself relaxing slightly. He really was rather nice, and in other circumstances she could imagine him to be very pleasant company.

A guided tour through the various outbuildings—a fascinating first for Gwayne—occupied the rest of their time on Murramai and then they were winging their way home. It was a relatively silent trip this time, though, as she set about attempting to put her confused thoughts in order.

Brad appeared from nowhere the moment they set foot on the verandah, making Regan's brows lift provokingly, and Gwayne colour at the undisguised inference. At such a time she wasn't interested in discounting Brad's unfounded theories. His enquiries regarding her welfare she answered as brightly as she could, but mentioned nothing of what had occurred at Murramai apart from her tour around the hub of the station. The other she preferred to keep to herself.

During dinner she was on tenterhooks lest Regan should deliberately bring the subject up, but fortunately he didn't. Whether out of consideration for her, or for some undisclosed reason of his own, Gwayne wasn't sure—she was too relieved to care. After the meal had been concluded and Regan and his aunt had left to discuss some matters relating to the shearers' pending arrival, the four of them spent a desultory evening playing darts and table tennis in the cedar-lined games room. A few hours of amusement and hilarity before Gwayne's earlier thoughts returned to relentlessly haunt her.

Once in bed she lay beneath her single covering sheet and found, after several determined efforts, that it was impossible to sleep and with a resigned shake of her head eventually gave up trying altogether. Perhaps a walk around the gardens would be all that was needed to put her mind at rest. It was that or a hot drink, but as she wasn't familiar with the layout of the kitchen and didn't want to be stumbling around in there in the middle of the night, she decided on the walk as the most suitable of the two. Shrugging into a short flower-patterned housecoat, she slid her feet in a pair of low-heeled sandals. At that hour there wasn't much likelihood of her bumping into anyone.

Down the steps she turned left and continued around to the back of the homestead, listening to the sounds of the night as she went; the continuous drone of cicadas, the muted call of a bird as it hunted, and away in the distance the eerie howl of a dingo for its mate. Something warm curled around her ankle, making her jump nervously, but on discovering it was only one of the cats which seemed to abound on the property she bent to give him a friendly scratch behind the ears and then moved on. She had no trouble seeing, the moon was full and clear in the star-sprinkled sky above, its rays tinting the water in the pool with a silvery gloss. If it hadn't been for the dressings on her back she would have been tempted to accept its shimmering invitation to ruffle the calm waters, but as it was she sighed and headed for a padded lounger some few feet distant.

For a time she lay quietly, her eyes closed as she sought to rationalise her feelings, but the short rasp of a lighter had them flashing open again and searching amongst the shadows. Near the gate leading to the yards she espied Regan's powerful figure, head bent over the flame he was applying to the tip of his cigarette, and Gwayne could feel her muscles tensing as she froze into immobility in the desperate hope that he would pass on without noticing her.

Dressed as she had last seen him at dinner in olive green pants and a straw-coloured silk knit shirt which made his bronzed skin appear even darker, he drew and captured her attention as if she was a hypnotised rabbit without a will of her own. There was a compelling maleness about him she seemed incapable of resisting and it was only when he was being deliberately provoking that she had a chance to override her wayward emotions in a show of rebellion—an intolerable situation and one which had her, yet again, berating herself soundly for allowing it to occur.

Almost as if he sensed the aura of anger which surrounded her, Regan now turned and stared disconcertingly in her direction, his eyes reflecting the same luminous light as the pool as he began pacing towards her with a lithe and leisurely stride.

'Were you waiting for me?' he quizzed dryly.

Gwayne clamped down on her escalating pulse and shook her head with what she hoped was disdainful rejection. 'No, I was seeking a little solitude, actually.'

But Regan evidently wasn't going to take the hint, because he calmly took a seat on the edge of the lounger and sent her a teasing glance.

'You didn't have that in your bedroom?'

'I couldn't sleep!' she flung at him irritably, and drew her legs beneath her to avoid his disquieting nearness as much as possible. 'What's your excuse?'

'For still being awake? I was making arrangements with Dan to have that bull trucked down from Murramai.' Those ebony-lashed eyes surveyed her intently. 'You were pretty hard on Simon today, weren't you?'

Gwayne wrapped her arms tightly about her midriff. The subject was still too sensitive within her own mind for her to want to discuss it. 'I don't think so,' she returned stiffly. 'After all, just because you choose to believe something, doesn't mean I have to automatically do the same.'

'Mmm, and that especially applies when you're being bloody-minded in revenge for all those years you had to spend in the orphanage, I suppose,' he derided.

'How dare you!' Gwayne came to her knees with her eyes blazing and her hand swinging violently for a lean brown cheek. 'What would you know about it anyway?'

An intercepting forearm effectively thwarted her attempt at physical retribution as Regan dropped his cigarette to the ground, and the next second she found both arms gripped ungently and him issuing the bleak warning, 'I wouldn't advise you to try that again if I were you, sweetheart. You might not find me quite so forbearing the next time you feel like indulging in a free-for-all!'

'Then leave me alone!' she ordered fiercely, struggling to break free. 'I didn't ask you to join me, and I certainly didn't ask for your opinion regarding my behaviour,' as she managed to slide her legs over the side of the lounger in a bid to gain her feet. 'You're nothing but a high-handed, interfering troublemaker!'

'Oh?' There was such a sarcastically questioning note in his exclamation that Gwayne's heart nervously missed a beat and then raced on tumultuously as she fought to stop him from pulling her back to the middle of the lounger. 'That being the case, I might as well live up to the part, mightn't I?' Grey eyes glittered baitingly down into hers.

Pinned by his hands on her upper arms, Gwayne moved her head in a frantic gesture when his mouth began lowering to hers. Fierily, she threatened, 'Let me go, Regan, or I'll scream so loud they'll hear me in Jeedara!'

'Scream away,' came the complacent invitation. 'I'll just tell everyone you arranged to meet me out here and then suffered an attack of cold feet. Dressed like you are, I don't anticipate any difficulty in making them believe me.'

Gwayne's breasts heaved with impotent anger. 'Why, you ... !'

'Troublemaker,' he filled in for her laconically before his lips fastened to hers in an explosive kiss which threatened to irrevocably overturn her puny defences.

Sensing the uncontrollable defection of her emotions, she twisted wildly to disrupt the searing contact. 'No! Stop it!' She strained away from him furiously. 'You're only doing this to get at Brad!'

Long lashes lifted slowly to reveal a warmly possessive gaze. 'Brad who?' he parried huskily, and slid his hands upwards to imprison her head between them.

Taken unawares by his reply, Gwayne disconcertingly realised she was actively responding to his renewed attack upon her senses and belatedly made an effort to convince him of her opposition. When pushing and pummelling against his rugged chest had no effect she changed her approach and purposefully grabbed two handfuls of his crisply curling hair. But having reached that far, to her despair and consternation, she could go no further. As Regan's persuasive mouth robbed her of the will to resist, so his exploring hands now sapped her desire to retaliate, and instead of fulfilling their original intention her fingers tangled capriciously within the dark thatch, all thought of reprisals evaporating.

Through the gossamer fineness of her attire Gwayne could feel every exciting plane and muscle of Regan's vital shape, and in a flushed and ecstatic haze she melted sensuously against him, offering only a low irresolute murmur of protest when his hand slipped beneath the wide neckline of her nightdress to close around a tautly swelling breast. He had the ability to arouse her like no other man ever had before and she responded to his caresses uninhibitedly, her skin burning from his touch, her senses whirling out of control. When he made a move away she knew a plunging feeling of disappointment and deprivation, then discovered his withdrawal had been occasioned so he could slide an arm beneath her knees and another about her back to swing her hard against his chest as he rose effortlessly to his feet.

Neither of them broke the electric silence as he strode with her towards the homestead. Gwayne doubted whether she could have done even had she wanted to. Her throat was tight and dry, her breathing raw and erratic. With her arms still linked about the firm column of his neck and her head resting weakly against his shoulder she sent a covert look upwards from beneath curling lashes, her vision centring on a tiny muscle flickering unsteadily beside the corner of his fascinating mouth.

Shouldering through the doorway into her room, Regan bent to deposit her gently on the bed, his lips meeting hers firmly but briefly, before he straightened and headed back the way they had just come.

Gwayne levered herself up on to one elbow, following his tall figure across the room with disbelieving eyes. Surely he wasn't going to leave her just like that! Didn't he intend to at least say *something*? She called after him in bewilderment.

'Regan ... ?'

Halfway to the door she heard him sigh as he stopped and dragged a hand roughly through his hair. He swung to face her, his brows arched enquiringly. 'Yes?'

'I—you ...' Her voice died away and, embarrassed, she began to fidget with one of the buttons on her housecoat, wishing she had left well enough alone.

Regan took a step towards the bed and then braked again, an almost tangible air of self-discipline emanating from him. 'Have you ever slept with Brad?' he demanded harshly.

Oh, God, was that why he thought she had accepted his intimate caresses so compliantly? Because she was used to such familiarities? Her eyes flew to his indignantly.

'No, I haven't!' she burst out. And just to make her position quite clear, 'I've never slept with any man!'

'Then I wouldn't suggest you delay my departure for very much longer,' he advised tautly. 'Otherwise you could find that's the last time you'll be able to make that claim.'

His meaning was plain enough and Gwayne flushed hotly, her gaze dropping before his. Feeling as she did she doubted that was a prediction she was in a position to repudiate right at the moment. When she lifted her eyes again he was gone, and she gave vent to a sigh that was half relieved and half disappointed. She had never been one to indulge in promiscuous affairs, but with Regan ... Unconsciously her thoughts wandered on, reliving those minutes when a shapely mouth had demanded, and masterful hands had overwhelmingly exhilarated.

Abruptly she rolled off the bed and began searching for her cigarettes. Dear God, what was the matter with her? She was as bad—if not worse—as she had accused Donna of being! Hadn't Brad warned her about ... ! Brad! Guilt washed over her like a gigantic tidal wave. How could she have forgotten him so readily, so *unconscientiously*? Lighting her cigarette, Gwayne drew on it deeply and sank down on the bed, her forehead creased and troubled.

There was enough friction between Brad and Regan already without her recklessly creating more. It was one thing to be attracted to their vibrant host, but something else again to even remotely suppose he was interested in anything other than a four-week casual flirtation. Besides, she shrugged, she owed her loyalty to Brad. He was the one who had brought her here, and he would be the one she returned to Sydney with. His cousin was a complication she didn't need!

Deliberately she steeled herself into dismissing any lingering thoughts regarding Regan and concentrated on her previous problem—the mystery of her parentage. To herself she could admit that there did appear to be quite a substantial amount of evidence to suppose that Simon Houghton could be her father, but no matter how strongly he and Regan tried to convince her to do so, there was no way she was going to concede such a relationship without positive proof.

As a child she had prayed so often for her mother to return that, when she hadn't, she had learnt to hide her feelings in this respect and to be extremely wary of showing them again. As much as she felt she would like to, it was impossible for her to accept Simon on the off-chance that he *might* be her father because it would be too much to bear if eventually that assumption was proved incorrect. She had to be absolutely sure first! Without anything definite to go on then as far as she was concerned the matter would have to remain static. A case of possible identity only, nothing more!

With a sigh she stubbed out her cigarette and slowly began removing her housecoat, hoping that if she did manage to sleep this time it would be dreamless. She had enough to worry about when she was awake, without experiencing problems when she was asleep as well!

During the next two days they saw little of Regan as all available hands took part in the shearing muster. Gradually the holding yards close by the woolshed were filled to capacity as mobs of heavily woolled sheep were brought in from all corners of the property, their complaining bleats disturbing the tranquil quiet, their churning feet sending clouds of red dust spiralling into the atmosphere.

As their opportunities for prospecting were denied them owing to the stockmen's need for the Range Rovers, Gwayne and her companions spent most of their daylight hours in and around the swimming pool or on the tennis court. With no further mention being made concerning the disclosures she had encountered at Murramai, Gwayne allowed the matter to settle into a convenient and composed little niche in her subconscious.

She had said nothing at all about it to either Brad or Donna—her most likely confidants—deeming it a futile exercise in view of the improbability of its ever being authenticated. Donna's reaction would no doubt have been one of pleasure for her friend and a bubbling inability to keep such information to herself, but it was Brad's suspected response which had been the greatest deterrent. Gwayne just couldn't envisage him receiving the news with any show of either joy or equanimity!

The arrival of the shearers heralded an even greater degree of activity about the homestead and on the third morning Gwayne gave in to her friend's demand that she accompany her to the shearing shed to watch the skilled process. Donna had spent almost the whole of her time there over the two preceding days—because that was where Regan was usually to be found, deduced Gwayne wryly, and surprisingly not a little caustically —but it was exactly for that same reason that she herself had refused to go when first invited. No matter how interested she was she didn't want Regan thinking she had any intention of succumbing to his dynamic masculinity a second time, and the best way to do that was to steer clear of him altogether. This particular morning, however, Donna had been insistent, and rather than arouse her suspicions Gwayne had finally consented to join her.

Naturally, Brad had some disgruntled words to say about their idea—shearing was nothing new to him—but as Donna was so determined he gave in with ill-grace and with Warren making an easy-going fourth they made their way across the compound shortly after breakfast.

Inside the shed strategically placed fans provided the shearers with some relief from the rapidly mounting heat as they went about their backbreaking work. To a man they were dressed in navy blue singlets and jeans, a sheep gripped between their knees, shears slicing deftly through the wool.

The belly wool was shorn first—being shorter and dirtier than the rest of the fleece—then the shears were brought up the neck and over the left shoulder to the front leg, followed by long sweeps along the side and over the back, turn, and the manoeuvre was completed by going down the neck, shoulder and last side, finishing at the right-hand leg. In less than two minutes the sheep was divested of its long fleece and released into a counting pen, and by the time the rouseabout had gathered and carried the wool to the sorting table where it was thrown out in a single layer, 'skirted'— any loose or dirty edges trimmed—and handed on to the wool classer, the shearer already had another animal pinned securely and the whole procedure began again.

Even as they stood watching Gwayne could sense Donna's restlessness and when, after only seeing another half dozen sheep pass through the pens, the other girl suggested, 'Come on, let's go and see the wool being pressed,' she understood why.

Regan was in that section of the shed talking to the shearing contractor, a big man with a friendly smile and easy manner who was introduced as Ray Dickson, and who genially answered all of Gwayne's interested questions as he went about his work.

Brad and Warren moved over to where an increasing number of bales were being stacked against the wall and sat down on the most convenient one, preparing to wait until the girls had exhausted their queries. Though in Brad's case, with unconcealed impatience and dissatisfaction. As always, he would have preferred to be somewhere his cousin wasn't.

Ray released another large bale from the press and began printing letters and numbers over it with the aid of stencils and heavy black marking paint.

'Those marks, Ray, what do they represent?' Gwayne's head tilted to one side enquiringly.

'Well,' he smiled, and indicated the top letters. 'R.D.F.—they're Regan's initials, and FAIRFAX DOWNS speaks for itself, of course. Next, the triple A denotes the quality of the wool, and the number shows how many bales of that particular type of wool there are. The other set of initials at the bottom are those of the agents it's to be shipped to. There's only a limited number of wool-broking houses, so it's not necessary to put their full names. Most of them are only known by their initials anyway.'

She nodded understandingly. 'I see. You've got it down to quite a fine art, haven't you?' with a laugh. Then, waving a hand towards a bin near the shearers, 'Would that first wool they take off be classified as triple A too?'

'Oh, my word, no,' he denied vigorously. 'All the

different grades are baled separately. There's triple A, double A, ram's wool, belly wool, first or second crutchings, and so on. There's more to it than just shearing the sheep and cramming as many fleeces as possible into each bale.'

Her eyebrows arched expressively and she smiled. 'So I'm beginning to realise. But with so many categories doesn't it become confusing when you're stamping them?'

At this Regan turned from where he had been answering a question of Donna's to make a faintly reproving sound. 'Branding, not stamping,' he advised lazily, and after her frowned incomprehension, 'A wool bale is always *branded*, never stamped.'

'Oh ...' Gwayne licked at her lips awkwardly and lifted a diffident shoulder. It wasn't so much his correction that was making her nervous, it was just that since the night of their visit to Murramai she had found it well nigh impossible to act naturally in his presence. 'I'm displaying my ignorance again, am I?' she somehow managed to pressure herelf into laughing lightly. 'I suppose you'll be accusing me of doubting Ray's ability next because I asked if he didn't find it confusing.'

As he and the rouseabout upended another overflowing bin into the press Ray chuckled. 'You weren't, I hope,' he quizzed.

'Heavens, no!' she smiled at him quickly. 'I only meant ...'

'That although she's developed the habit of doing that to herself, she doesn't where others are concerned,' was Regan's drawling insertion—a remark which had Gwayne sending him an angry glare and Donna eyeing them both perplexedly.

At that moment even Brad's somewhat petulant,

'For goodness' sakes, haven't you two seen enough yet?' came as a relief and Gwayne turned to nod at him eagerly.

'Just about,' she smiled.

Without any hesitation Brad started for the door with a reluctant Donna following with Warren, but when Gwayne would have gone after them a hand on her arm halted her after only a few steps and she swung round apprehensively.

'By the way ...' Regan's white teeth gleamed in the darkness of his face, causing Gwayne's pulse to rocket dizzily, 'how did Brad take the news regarding your possible connection with Simon? You must have chosen a very delicate method of telling him as I fully expected to be able to hear his roar of disapproval. Brad usually takes the mention of any entitlement to property or money as a personal affront.'

Gwayne gave a passable imitation of an indifferent shrug but couldn't quite hold his gaze and pretended an absorbed interest in what Ray was doing with the wool press. A relentless hand spanning her jaw and tilting her head backwards destroyed that stratagem, however.

'The penny's beginning to drop,' his lips curved wryly. 'You haven't yet mentioned it to him at all, have you?'

'There—um—there wasn't any point,' she evaded, and hastily pulled away from his disconcerting touch. 'It can never be verified.'

'But Simon's intending to give it a damned good try, sweetheart, and what if he's successful, hmm? What then?'

She hadn't allowed herself to think that far ahead. 'Well, I—I won't have any choice, I guess.'

'You don't think it would make things easier if you

at least gave him a hint of what could be coming?'

'I—I don't know really. I haven't given it all that much consideration.'

Regan's slanting look was totally disbelieving. 'Liar! You know as well as I do what Brad's reaction is likely to be.' His eyes narrowed slightly. 'But if that's the obstacle, I'm quite willing to tell him for you.'

'Oh, I'm sure you are, and take great pleasure from doing so too, I've no doubt!' she gibed recklessly, her desire to prove she was unaffected by his presence overcoming her discretion. 'But no, thanks, *if* it's necessary for anyone to tell him, I will. There is such a thing as allegiance, you know!'

An indistinct epithet and the corners of his mouth levelled ominously. 'Oh, I know all right,' he assured her icily. 'It just comes as something of a surprise that you do. I seem to remember you were willing enough to put pleasure before loyalty a few nights ago.'

Gwayne crimsoned at the suggestion and if there hadn't been so many potential onlookers she would have taken great pleasure from slapping his face—hard! As it was her hands clenched tightly at her sides and her eyes sparkled fiercely.

'Why, you—you ...!' she spluttered, inwardly cursing the feminine restraint which prevented her from voicing what she felt like saying. 'I wish to heaven we'd never come here!'

'Because you received a little in kind?' he queried satirically. 'Well, maybe you should have thought of that before you started crediting me with your own ill-conceived notions. I fight fire with fire, sweetheart, so if you don't like getting burnt, don't keep setting light to short fuses!' Which was probably good advice, allowed Gwayne ironically, although not without some asperity. 'And for your information,' Regan continued

just as bitingly, 'the only reason I suggested *my* telling
Brad was that I happen to know him a little better
than you do. His reaction is likely to be anything but
endearing! But if that's the way you want it then go
right ahead. Don't let me stop you!' He paused momentarily and his glance was unpleasantly corrosive. 'Just
don't come running to me when the going gets rough
and you realise you've bitten off more than you can
chew, that's all!'

Under his openly derisive regard Gwayne's chin lifted
challengingly, her figure stiff with anger and indignation. 'I wouldn't dream of it!' she blazed. 'In fact, if
you hadn't seen fit to mention it, I doubt it would even
have occurred to me! As much as this may shock you,
I happen to have survived very well until now without any help from the all-powerful Fairfax family—
especially one particular member—and I don't anticipate any trouble in the future doing the same. Brad's
attitude to such a disclosure might possibly leave something to be desired,' a small admission to make in the
face of what she was about to say next, 'but I can
assure you it could never be quite so grating and un-
palatable as yours is at the best of times. You're too
ruthlessly arrogant by half for my liking!'

'Is that so?' The words were only just above a
whisper, but Gwayne was shiveringly aware that was
due to a rigid self-control being imposed and not to a
lack of feeling. 'Well, there's quite a few home truths I
wouldn't mind expounding for your edification too,
sweetheart, only I hardly think now is the time or the
place,' Regan ground out contemptuously. 'Instead, I
suggest you would do well to ensure you keep right out
of my way for the rest of your stay, otherwise you just
might find yourself paying an extremely high price for
what was obviously intended as a cheap holiday!'

Having been both sharply rebuked for using the woolshed as the venue for her stinging remarks, and bluntly reminded that she was, after all, still a guest on Fairfax Downs, there wasn't much Gwayne could do except comply with what little poise was left to her.

'That suits me fine,' she told him coolly, albeit a trifle jerkily, but couldn't avoid adding a sarcastic, 'Providing you mean to abide by that suggestion as well, of course!'

'You can count on it!' Regan's mouth tightened inflexibly.

An imperceptible nod and Gwayne turned on her heel, her composure frayed but her head held defensively high. Nothing would please her more than to have him keep at a distance. Or would it . . . ?

CHAPTER SEVEN

THEY didn't see Regan again that day. He was missing from the dining room at both lunch and dinner time, although there was a perfectly good reason for his absence from the latter meal—his aunt informing them that he had left for the Halfords' some time during the afternoon—a fact which caused Gwayne some moments of unexpected discomfort until she put a severe clamp on her capricious emotions by continually reminding herself that it at least had the effect of keeping Brad in a good mood.

Time and again her thoughts had returned to Regan's suggestion that she should give Brad 'a hint of what might be coming', but on each occasion she had shied away from voicing such a revelation. If they hadn't been planning to remain for another two weeks she would have dismissed the idea out of hand, but if Simon *was* making a studied effort to confirm their relationship as Regan intimated then it was more than possible that others would come to hear about it—she had heard too often how quickly news travelled with the aid of the outback radio 'talk' sessions—and Brad certainly wouldn't be pleased, nor would it be fair, if he was one of the last to know. All in all Gwayne found herself with quite a problem and, to make her all the more uneasy, it wasn't one of her creation either!

After dinner the four of them had played a few light-hearted games of table tennis, but now that Donna and Warren had gone for a stroll in the gardens before turning in, Gwayne thought it unlikely that a better opportunity would present itself for her to advise Brad of the details, and particularly since he was in a decidedly cheerful frame of mind.

As he released her lips from one long passionate kiss to begin a series of feather-light ones across her cheeks, she swallowed nervously and eased gently out of his embrace, conscious as she did so that she was secretly a little pleased to have an excuse to call a halt. She didn't know why, but in some indescribable way his kisses had begun to pall.

Pulling at a stray lock of hair in an uncharacteristically agitated motion, she returned his slightly frowning look apologetically. 'I'm sorry, Brad, but there's something I have to tell you,' she excused her action in an anxious tone.

He clasped his hands behind his head and leant back against the hide couch they were sharing, his eyes suddenly watchful. 'Such as?'

Gwayne began with the query, 'You remember when I went to Simon Houghton's property with Regan the other day?' and after his perfunctory nod, went on, 'Well, I won't bore you with all the details, and although it's strictly unproven as yet, there is some evidence to suggest that he . . .' she took a deep breath and dropped her gaze to the fingers which were now twining together apprehensively in her lap before concluding with a rush, 'that he might be my father.'

There was a rasping sound remarkably like a snarl, and then she couldn't believe her ears when he jeered, 'So what's this . . . the brush-off? I suppose I'm not considered good enough for you now!'

'No! That's not it at all!' she denied vehemently.

'Isn't it?' He didn't sound at all convinced. 'Then why else have you been cooling off towards me, eh?'

Gwayne licked at her lips and prepared to defend

herself as best she could. 'But I haven't been . . .'

'Oh, yes, you have, and you know it, so don't try playing me for an idiot, Gwayne!' he interjected sarcastically. 'Directly we arrived on Fairfax Downs you started to change. Discovering you've got a wealthy father just gives you an added incentive.'

'Apart from the fact that I don't know for sure yet whether he is my father or not, is that obnoxious suggestion the only comment you have to make?' she demanded scornfully.

One corner of his mouth curled up in a satirical sneer. 'What did you expect me to say? Congratulations?' He gave a disparaging snort. 'For what? So you can give chase to my filthy rich cousin with a clear conscience now that you're right up there in his league?'

Gwayne's nervousness was rapidly being replaced by anger. 'No, I thought I might have been able to discuss the matter with you,' she snapped. 'But I should have known better, apparently. You've got such a damned phobia about Regan that it blinds you to everything else! Don't forget that your personality underwent quite a sudden change too immediately we hit the place, Brad. You're not the person I knew in Sydney either!'

'So now it's all my fault, is it?'

'Fault! Who's talking about fault?' She ran trembling fingers across her forehead as if attempting to dismiss an unpleasant dream. 'I would be happy if I could just convince you that I have no intention of chasing after your cousin, and that I couldn't care less if I was in his league, as you put it, or not!' Her eyes held his frustratedly and she made an effort to return to her original topic. 'Aren't you even interested to hear why Simon believes I might be his daughter?'

Brad shrugged with a graphic indifference. 'Not particularly. I gather there must be a strong case or else you wouldn't have mentioned it, and you did say you wouldn't bore me with details,' he reminded her derisively.

In a flash Gwayne was on her feet, fuming. 'Then as it's evidently such a trial for you, perhaps I shouldn't inflict my presence on you either!'

'I suppose that's as good an excuse as any.'

'For what?'

'For getting yourself out of an uncomfortable situation,' he elucidated coldly. 'Being able to conveniently lay the blame for our blow-up at my door leaves you free to pursue more profitable relationships, doesn't it?'

Gwayne's eyes rose ceilingwards in despair. 'You really do have a one-track mind, don't you, Brad? Luckily, though, it doesn't run parallel with mine, and if you weren't so engaged with your own prejudices you would have realised that long ago. There's absolutely no reason for us to be quarrelling over this, you know. Nothing's been verified,' she stressed persuasively.

But Brad wasn't about to yield his fixed stance and made no move to meet her halfway, merely raking over her with hostile eyes. 'And if it is, what do you suppose will happen then?'

'I—well, whatever happens, there's no cause for it to make any difference to us, is there?'

'You think not?' he uttered a short bark of sardonic laughter. 'Well, let me put you wise, honey. Courting heiresses just isn't my scene, and I've got no desire to be pointed out as the local fortune-hunter, thanks all the same!'

'Oh, but that's ridiculous!' she exclaimed incredulously. Was this really the same man who had been kissing her so ardently only a few short minutes ago? 'The trouble with you is, you're an inverted snob. If you can't have money yourself then you take pride in refusing to have anything to do with those who have.'

Brad swung to his feet and thrust his hands into the pockets of his pants, his head pushed adamantly forward as he rasped, 'Call it what you like, but that's the way it is and that's the way it's going to stay. The minute you accept Simon Houghton as your father we're through ... finished ... kaput! Got it?'

Even as he was biting out those last words he was brushing past her and before Gwayne could recover from the shock his bitter sentiments had created, he had already left the room. Feeling slightly weak at the knees, and totally fogged in her mind, she sank down on to the couch again with a hand pushing distractedly through her curly hair.

Good lord, had she really heard him right? Did he honestly think he could issue that kind of an ultimatum over something so important? Choose him, or a father, but not both! She couldn't believe it. He was either insufferably egotistical—which she just couldn't credit —or else he was deliberately putting her in a position where there was only one decision she could make. And that, now she had put it into thought, did tend to make more sense.

It wasn't the first time during their acquaintanceship that she had thought she'd detected a faint flair for self-pity in Brad's nature, and if that was the case then this last stipulation of his could be a prime example of it. It could also explain why he had agreed to bring them to Fairfax Downs when he so obviously disliked the property. Surely if that had been anyone else they would have greeted the suggestion that they spend their holidays in a place they found so disagreeable with a flat refusal, no matter what persuasions were used?

The longer she thought about it the more certain Gwayne became that she was correct in her deduction. Not that it made her feel any better, but at least it enabled her to put things into some sort of perspective. Even if Simon wasn't her father there could never be anything further between Brad and herself. Who could tell what would be his next condition for their continuing friendship? But, in the meantime, she would have to walk a very fine line for the rest of her stay. First Regan, and now Brad, she mused ruefully with a shake of her head. Another couple of weeks like the last one and she could find herself at odds with *everyone* on the property before she left.

'Thank heavens, I've been trying to sneak a private word with you all day,' whispered Donna the following afternoon as they seated themselves in the shade of the trees and prepared to watch their companions thrash out a no-nonsense game of singles on the tennis court. 'What on earth is up with Brad? He reminds me of a smoking volcano—one that's about to blow its top at any second!'

'It's a long story,' Gwayne shrugged. Was there any use in prevaricating? 'Are you sure you want to hear it?'

Donna responded with an extremely ironic look and a dry, 'What do you think?' which edged Gwayne into reluctant laughter.

'Okay, you asked for it. Don't say I didn't warn you,' she smiled, and launched into a brief, but concise as possible resumé of events for her friend's benefit. When she had finished she sighed and glanced sideways. 'Well, what do you think?'

'I think it's absolutely marvellous! And I can guess what it must mean to you that you might have found one of your parents,' Donna exclaimed happily. 'Is he very nice?'

'That's somewhat difficult to judge on the strength of a single afternoon's visit,' Gwayne grinned. 'But yes, I do think he might be.'

'And he's making all the necessary enquiries?'

'So Regan says.'

Donna gave her a gentle nudge with her elbow. 'I'm more excited about it than you are,' she chuckled—a sound that died quickly when her glance ranged over the two on the court and an incredulous frown appeared. 'Yet Brad had the hide to suggest you should choose between them. He must have rocks in his head! You need someone like that about as much as you need a raincoat in the middle of the desert. If I were you, I'd tell him to get lost right here and now!'

'I still have to get back to Sydney, don't forget,' she was reminded wryly.

'Maybe, maybe not. If all goes well you could be heading off in an entirely different direction.'

'Oh, no, nothing could possibly be settled in that short a time.' Gwayne looked across at her friend half nervously. 'Could it?'

'I suppose that depends on how much effort you're willing to expend. But if money's no object ... it's feasible,' Donna grinned encouragingly.

Until now Gwayne had refused to contemplate such an eventuality, but Donna's optimism was catching and for the first time she found herself actually considering the outcome of Simon's search with a ray of hope instead of pushing it dismally to the farthest reaches of her mind. However, her hopefulness wasn't so strong as yet that she could continue discussing her future possibilities with impassivity and in order to divert Donna's attention she deliberately changed to the subject she thought most likely to succeed, even though it was one she would have preferred to leave well alone.

'Talking about prospects ... how are yours progressing with our host?' she made herself smile, a widening of her lips which Donna would have recognised as being brittle, not mindful, if she had paid closer attention.

But Donna was already pulling a rueful grimace and confessing, 'Not very well, I'm sorry to say. Oh, he's always courteous, obliging, and complimentary,' which was more than could be said for his treatment of herself, thought Gwayne tartly, 'but I still get the feeling I'm attempting the impossible. I get the impression that neighbour of his, Arleen Halford, must have a stronger hold on him than I imagined.' She waved one hand furiously in front of her face to discourage a persistent fly before musing, 'And that's something of a surprise really. I wouldn't have thought he was the type to fall for someone so cold and supercilious.'

'Maybe she's not when they're alone together,' tautly.

'Mmm, and maybe a leopard can change its spots too,' Donna suggested dryly. 'Who do you think you're kidding? *Miss* High-and-Mighty Halford ...' She paused to insert an incredulous, 'Do you know what she replied when Brad asked her that night we came back from prospecting how come she'd reverted to her maiden name? Well, I'll tell you. It's because she "doesn't like to be reminded of the worst three years of her life",' with cutting mimicry. 'I'll bet her poor damned ex-husband doesn't care to remember them either!' A moment's silence and then she laughed. 'I'm really getting worked up today, aren't I? Anyway, to return to what I was saying—Arleen Halford is such a coldblooded specimen I doubt even the ultra-masculine Regan Fairfax could warm her up.'

A far cry from how he affected *her*, Gwayne reflected anguishedly. He only had to touch her for all her emotions to flare into feverish turmoil. Deep in her own thoughts she was vaguely aware of Donna saying something else and shook her head quickly to clear it.

'I'm sorry, my mind must have wandered off for a moment,' she apologised self-consciously, and added 'along a disastrous course' for her own benefit. 'What was that you said?'

'I asked your opinion,' Donna smiled.

'About what?' Her thoughts were refusing to obediently come to order.

'Gwayne!' The ejaculation was a mildly exasperated remonstrance. 'We were talking about Arleen Halford ... remember?'

'Oh, yes—sorry. Well, perhaps that's the way he prefers his girl-friends to be.'

Donna wrinkled her nose in mock disgust. 'You're hopeless! How could you possibly think that about someone like Regan?'

'Why not?' Gwayne retorted. 'Just because he happens to have an excess of money and good looks it doesn't make him perfect, you know!'

'Wow!' Donna grinned broadly and shook her fingers as if to cool them. 'That was a pretty severe dig, wasn't it? Anyone would think it was you getting the knock-back from him, not me!'

Uncomfortably, the comment was too charged with overtones Gwayne would rather have ignored and she almost choked in her anxiety to squash such an assumption once and for all.

'I should live so long! He's the last man I'd be interested in!'

'For crying out loud, why? What's he done to rile you that much?'

Aware that she was perhaps coming on a little too strong in response to what had, when all was said and done, only been meant as a joking remark, Gwayne took a couple of deep steadying breaths and smiled wryly.

'Sorry, but he just rubs me the wrong way.' And on noticing her friend's frown, 'There's no call for you to worry, though, I do the same to him too, apparently. Only yesterday he advised me to stay out of his way from now on for my own good.' She wasn't really being fair by only telling part of the story, Gwayne knew, but right at the present she had more worrying things on her mind.

'But—but why would he say that?' Donna gasped. 'He would have to have a reason, surely.'

Oh, he'd had one of those all right. She had just thrown his offer of help very impetuously back into his face, together with some extremely rash insinuations, Gwayne recollected gloomily. Aloud she made light of it.

'I—er—said some things which he apparently took exception to.'

'Strong exception by the sound of it,' Donna grinned. 'Exactly what were these—um—*things* you said?'

'Does it matter?' Gwayne shrugged with apparent negligence and, seeking to change the subject yet again, announced, 'By the way, I've been told there's a gymkhana coming up quite soon on the Halfords' property. John Foster, the doctor I saw at the hospital, was saying that everyone goes.'

The idea obviously caught Donna's fancy. 'Us too?' she asked eagerly.

'If we want to,' Gwayne nodded.

'And how do we get there?'

'By car, I gather.'

Donna's happy look faded slightly. 'Oh, that's a pity, I was looking forward to having a jaunt in that plane of Regan's. Still, it can't be helped, I suppose,' she cheered again almost immediately. 'I've always wanted to go to one of these country turn-outs, and now it seems my opportunity has arrived at long last, so I won't complain about our method of transport. How long will it take to get there? Does Brad know?'

Gwayne's eyes flew to his wiry figure on the court, watching momentarily as he smashed an easy shot hopelessly past the base line—his angry mood clearly wasn't doing anything for his game—and then hunched her shoulders briefly.

'I expect so,' she sighed. 'Although to be quite honest I haven't even mentioned it to him yet. What with all that's happened, it completely slipped my mind until a few minutes ago.'

'I'm not surprised, you must have had plenty to occupy your thoughts. It's not every day of the week you discover a father who's been missing for over twenty years.' Donna sent Gwayne an interested look. 'Will he be at the gymkhana as well?'

'I should imagine so. Why?'

'Because I want to meet him, of course, dummy!' Donna laughed. 'This could be the man who's going to deprive me of a flatmate.'

'Oh, please!' Gwayne held up a restraining hand. 'Don't let's start taking anything for granted, it's all too inconclusive at the moment. Couldn't we talk about something else?'

A request Donna acceded to understandingly. 'Okay. Perhaps we ought to concentrate on what we're going to do about Brad instead. Something tells me he's not exactly going to be the life and soul of the party for the next two weeks.'

'How about a suggestion to the effect that we cut short our visit?' proposed Gwayne.

'No fear!' was the decisive veto. 'I don't know about you, but by hook or by crook, *I* intend going to that do at the Halfords' even though it will mean putting up with dear Arleen's presence.'

'Mmm, there is that to consider, isn't there?' Gwayne's mobile lips tilted wryly. 'But have you thought that—Brad himself may decide it's time we left?'

A triumphant look implanted itself on Donna's face. 'He can't!' she chortled. 'We all made a decision— remember?—before we started the trip. If there was any conflict of interests we would put it to a vote and the majority rules. Warren will want to stay for this gymkhana, I'm sure of that, so Brad will be outvoted by three to one.'

'The way he's been acting today makes me doubt whether Brad's all that interested in doing anything democratically. He might just up and leave without conferring with any of us,' Gwayne reluctantly intimated her worst fears.

Donna's immediate reaction was an indignantly expostulated, 'He wouldn't dare!' but which she followed with a slower, amending, 'Although, on second thoughts, maybe he would. He does seem to get some unpredictably black moods up here, doesn't he? I'm beginning to regret having introduced you to him.'

'Now you're the one who's being an idiot,' Gwayne admonished with a grin. 'It's hardly your fault that he has this fixation with regard to Regan and Fairfax Downs.'

'No, but ... oh, hell, what a mess!' the other girl

sighed out her despair. 'You know Regan's said we could use the Range Rover again now if we want to?' Gwayne nodded and she continued, 'Well, Brad was saying yesterday that he wanted us to try our luck out at Amethyst Creek again before too long.'

'So?'

'It could make it unpleasant for you to spend a whole day in his company if he's going to carry on as he has today.'

'But I'm afraid our relationship is likely to become even more strained if I *don't*,' Gwayne countered with misgiving.

'Considering his peevish attitude, would that bother you terribly?'

'Probably not, under other circumstances, but we are guests here and that tends to make a difference,' Gwayne pointed out, then wondered if she shouldn't have thought of that more often in her dealings with their host.

A thought that was to return many times in the ensuing days as Brad's moodiness increased. One day he would be full of reproachful self-pity, the next angry and impossible to communicate with. Their second trip to the creek was depressing from start to finish, and not even Brad's own discovery of a glorious specimen of deep and flawless colour wedged into a crevice amongst the rocks had the ability to dispel his bad humour.

He found fault with everything Gwayne did or didn't do, and by the time they returned to the homestead— fortunately not quite so late this time—she was inwardly vowing that it was the very last prospecting venture she would be accompanying him on. Twelve hours' unmitigated carping was more than enough for anyone to have to undergo!

From then on she spent as much time as she could riding Puppet in the paddock. Her wrist was fully recovered now and her back almost so. It also gave her a chance to escape Brad's increasingly malicious comments because, of course, he had flatly refused to help with any further instructions. Fortunately Warren had no such reservations and although nowhere as experienced, he did at least have a good grounding in the fundamentals. Donna came with them most times—not to ride, as she contended that her only attempt had been a case of once too often for her liking—and watched from a comfortable position beneath the trees as she kept them amused with her running commentary.

One afternoon early in the fourth week, while the others were still spending a leisurely few hours beside the pool—Brad included for a change—Gwayne slipped away from them unobtrusively and hurried to change her clothes. Having felt quite capable in her handling of Puppet for some days now she had promised herself the treat of discovering what lay beyond that single confining paddock where her lessons had been taking place. She would have preferred to ask Warren to go with her, but as Donna couldn't, or wouldn't, ride she hadn't considered it fair to expect her friend to suffer Brad's doubtful companionship on her own while they were gone.

It was a beautiful day, hot but not oppressively so, the landscape still magnificently colourful, the sky an uninterrupted expanse of sun-drenched blue. Settling her hat firmly on her fiery tresses, Gwayne swung into the saddle and heeled the gelding out of the yard, her spirits lifting, her sherry brown eyes shining with expectation.

Once safely clear of the compound and heading east

she experimentally guided Puppet through his paces again and smiled happily to find herself automatically anticipating his responses. Twisting round to look over her shoulder she saw that the homestead was shrinking into the distance and she set a course for the meandering line of trees away in front of her, presuming their presence to signify water of some sort.

The ride across the plains was deceptively long, however, and by the time Gwayne reached the beckoning fingers of welcome shade created by the first of the trees she had slowed her mount from a canter to a walk and was fanning her hat coolingly before her face. As they picked their way carefully through the undergrowth she could make out the glint of sunlight on water directly in front of them and she urged Puppet forward more quickly, only to bring him to a halt a few moments later when the scrub thinned and she could sit and stare with widening and wondering eyes.

The last thing she had expected to see was a lagoon, and especially not one covered with giant waterlilies up to a foot wide in diameter, their delicately tinted petals of mauve, pink, white, and a touch of blue, opening radiantly beneath the golden sun. Amongst their profusion sailed a pair of pink-eared ducks and just visible on the far side was the snake-like head and neck of a darter as it searched through the water for a fish to spear with its long beak. The area was evidently a haven for many forms of birdlife and after silently watching the arrival of a number of spoonbills and red-eyed diamond doves, Gwayne skirted around the edge of the area so as not to disturb them and continued on her way.

It was impossible not to alarm some, though, she found a while later when a flock of budgerigars took to the air in protest at their arrival, giving an incredible display of their precise formation flying as they wheeled and turned as one, and always at high speed. In fact, as Gwayne discovered and followed the course of a winding creek, she was to see a greater variety of birds than she would have believed possible; small crimson and orange chats, butcherbirds and thornbills, red-backed parrots and crested pigeons, wrens, peewees, and cockatiels—all converging on the abundant feed provided in one form or another by the fertilising rains.

A little further on, as the creek degenerated into a succession of oxbow billabongs and shallow waterholes the trees became less numerous, giving a panoramic view of the plains between each sheltering stand, but when it appeared that she was travelling towards less and less hospitable country Gwayne decided it might be time to retrace her steps. A check of her watch showed she had, amazingly, been gone for over two hours and she swiftly changed direction. No doubt her absence would have been noted by now and she really hadn't intended to be away for so long.

Urging Puppet into a smooth distance-consuming gallop, she had almost reached the trees surrounding the source of the creek when movement to the west of her caught Gwayne's attention and she stopped in order to try and make out what it was. However, while on her head not even the wide brim of her hat was a match for the brilliant rays of a descending sun and she perforce had to hold it forward in her hand in order to screen as much of the fierce glare as she could. Now it was easier to see what had caused that momentary distraction.

A large sprawling mob of sheep was being moved in the general direction of the homestead—another batch for the shearers, she deduced—by two leisurely horsemen and their indefatigable dogs. About to resume moving herself, Gwayne paused when one of the riders abruptly broke away from the other and began galloping towards her. The big grey stallion closed the gap rapidly and then she was being very thoroughly surveyed by a familiar pair of dusky-framed, ash-coloured eyes.

'What's up? Where are the others?' Regan asked immediately. Or perhaps 'demanded' would have been more accurate.

It was the first time he had spoken directly to her since their confrontation in the woolshed and Gwayne found she was no nearer to controlling her emotions now than she had ever been when alone in his presence, and she responded stiltedly.

'They're—they're probably still in the pool,' she said.

'The lagoon, you mean?'

Suddenly she realised that he believed it to have been a signal when she had raised her hat in her hand and, feeling extremely foolish for having inadvertently interrupted his work, she explained with a conciliatory but self-conscious smile, 'No, I meant at the house. I'm sorry if you thought I was trying to attract your attention, because I was actually only trying to shade my eyes.' She squinted into the full force of the sun as if to verify her words. 'It's impossible to see anything out that way otherwise.'

Regan's brows drew thunderously close. 'Are you telling me you're here on your own?'

'Yes,' she nodded briefly, not a little pleased with herself. 'I wanted to—er—see some more of the property and I thought it would be a good opportunity to put into practice what I'd learnt in the paddock.'

'Did you? Then perhaps you would also be good

enough to tell me who the hell gave you permission?'
he rapped.

Bristling at the autocratic tone, Gwayne presented
him with a rebellious countenance. 'I wasn't aware any
permission was necessary!' she retaliated stormily.

'Only one of many things you're not aware of, I'm
sure,' was his countering sarcasm. 'But for your information, we have more to do with our time than to
spend it searching for headstrong females whose only
wish is to test their riding ability!'

'In that case, you have no worries at all, have you?'
she gibed. 'Because I am not now, nor was I at any
time this afternoon, likely to become lost. I may not
have been born in the outback, but I'm not such a
complete fool that I didn't make sure I could find my
way home again. Surprise, surprise!' she jeered lightly.
'I know exactly where I am and where I'm heading!'

'Excellent,' he applauded, but with heavy overtones
of facetiousness rather than praise. 'And if you'd found
out you weren't so competent as you believed and had
been thrown and hurt, then what?'

'Well, I—I ...' Her cheeks grew pink. Quite frankly
she hadn't given it a thought. 'I suppose Puppet would
have sounded the alarm by returning home without
me.'

Regan's expressive brows peaked aggravatingly.
'Would he? He might look extremely intelligent, but
why do you think he's called what he is, hmm?' And
without waiting for an answer, he enlightened her sardonically, 'Because he's obedient and reliable. But
don't expect initiative—he hasn't any! If you fell off he
would merely wait for you to remount ... and that
applies whether you were able to or not!'

'Oh!' Gwayne hunched one shoulder in a depreca-
tory gesture. 'Then perhaps you should have told us

that when you suggested we use Puppet for our lessons,' she retorted bitter-sweetly.

'There wasn't any need. Brad already knows better than to take any of the horses without checking with me first.' Unexpectedly his teeth gleamed in a lazy taunting smile. 'Or haven't you been speaking to him of late?'

'As if you don't know!' Gwayne's temper accelerated alarmingly, along with her heart rate. 'But thanks for reminding me it's all your damned fault anyway!' she flared unreasonably. Anything to repel the calamitous effects that smile was creating.

When she would have wheeled Puppet away an inexorable hand clamped down on to the reins to prevent her. 'Now just you hold on, young lady, while we set things straight!' Regan ordered arbitrarily. 'Although you may not be finding Brad's behaviour acceptable, I'm as sure as hell not going to have you railing at *me* as the cause of his infantile conduct!'

An attitude Gwayne couldn't really contest, but with Puppet—unfortunately as amenable as ever—standing close beside the grey and thereby forcing her leg into unsettling contact with Regan's powerfully muscled one, she purposely disregarded truth in favour of a protective impudence.

'I'd be interested to hear just how you propose to stop me,' she invited, her eyes provokingly wide.

All too swiftly a long-fingered hand was grasping the nape of her neck and forcibly tilting her head backwards as Regan leant towards her.

'This seems to have proved successful on a number of previous occasions, wouldn't you agree?' he mocked, and set his mouth to hers with a dominance which all too competently obliterated every thought from Gwayne's mind except for the insurmountable desire that he should continue his passionate arousal of her deepest emotions.

She knew now why Brad's embraces had lost their appeal so precipitately, and why his changed demeanour—apart from a certain annoyance—had worried her so little. Unknowingly she had altered too, only in a far more devastating fashion. She had fallen head over heels in love with his tantalising, tormenting cousin!

In his own good time Regan lifted his head slowly— Gwayne would have liked to persuade herself, unwillingly—but he didn't immediately set her free. In point of fact his compelling lips were still only inches away from hers and she could feel his breath warm against her tingling skin when he drawled,

'Point taken?'

Gwayne drew a shuddering breath and closed her eyes in order to hide her despair. 'Point taken,' she agreed huskily, knowing she would be all kinds of a fool if she let herself believe that kiss had involved any other feelings besides surface ones where he was concerned.

'Shall we go?'

At last he freed her and Gwayne's eyelids flew swiftly open again to find him indicating to westward, and all her senses rebelled at the idea of accompanying him to the homestead. She needed time in which to reassemble the shattered fragments of her self-control.

'No!' she rebuffed the suggestion vibrantly, and then followed it with an almost pleading, 'I—I'd rather go the same way as I came, if you don't mind.'

'You already know my feelings on that score,' he shook his head in exasperation.

'And now you know *mine*!' she retorted desperately, and with due deliberation began easing Puppet away.

The stallion responded to Regan's heeled command so quickly that Gwayne didn't have a chance to put more than a few feet between them before a hand was back on her reins.

'I think you'll find it less humiliating if you ride back to the house than if I lead you back,' she was advised dryly. But it was no less a warning for all that and her hopes took a dejected tumble.

'All right, all right, I've got the message!' she accepted her defeat acidly.

'I doubt it,' Regan returned with a surprising laziness, his smile heartbreakingly attractive. 'But there's always tomorrow, isn't there, sweetheart?'

Somewhere, somehow, he had lost her, but Gwayne wasn't in any mood for enigmas and merely angled him a disgruntled glance before urging her mount to a faster gait in order to keep pace with the grey. Regan sat a horse as if born in the saddle—which he probably very nearly had been, she added caustically—and she needed all her concentration to ensure she didn't disgrace herself. The thought did flash through her mind that he could have been testing her himself, but there was no time to dwell on the matter during that brisk gallop to catch up to Les and the sheep before they reached the homestead.

Back in the stable yard once the heavily fleeced animals had been efficiently herded into the holding pens, Gwayne handed Puppet over to Sam with a smile and had no choice but to accompany Regan through the compound and up to the house. An event which was becoming quite a habit, she mused ruefully.

'You know, I'm inclined to agree with Brad,' he angled her a fathomless glance as he shut the gate after they had passed into the gardens.

Suspicious as always when he mentioned the other man she eyed him warily. 'About what?'

'About you being a natural when it comes to riding. You're extremely good for someone with such limited experience.'

Praise from the master was praise indeed and Gwayne's cheeks blushed with becoming colour. 'You mean, I actually did everything right?' she laughed self-consciously.

'Oh, I don't know I would say that exactly,' he smiled gently down at her. 'But they're certainly only minor errors you're making and easily corrected with practice.'

'In other words, I should stick to the paddock,' wryly.

'Not at all,' he disallowed softly. 'I'm suggesting your efforts require a little polish applied to them.'

She sighed disconsolately. 'I don't think Warren would know how.'

'No ... but I do.'

Gwayne's eyes opened wide and she stared at him doubtfully. 'Are you offering to teach me yourself?' she probed.

One corner of his mouth twitched humorously. 'So it would seem.'

'I—why ...' Gwayne was flustered and didn't quite know what to say. On the one hand there was nothing she would like better, but on the other ... ? Feeling as she did wouldn't she only be asking for trouble by deliberately putting herself into such close proximity to him? She dragged her hat from her head, ran a slightly unsteady hand through her hair, and began to flatten the brim industriously between her fingers.

'Well?'

'I appreciate your offer very much,' she murmured carefully, keeping her eyes glued to her agitated hands. 'But I'm sorry, I can't accept.'

'Because of Brad?' Regan's voice was a shade cooler, a fraction less tolerant.

'Yes,' she lied miserably. 'You know how—how he would feel about it.'

There was a muffled ejaculation, halfway between a curse and a harsh disparagement, and then he expelled a long oppressed sigh. 'It's your decision,' he granted with what seemed to Gwayne to be an indifferent flexing of wide shoulders.

'Yes,' she whispered again in acknowledgment, but could only meet his silvery gaze fleetingly.

It wasn't even as if it was a decision she *wanted* to make; it was just an expedient one so she could guard her turbulent feelings. It would be all too mortifying if he ever discovered towards whom her wayward emotions were really directed!

In silence they made their way to the homestead and parted company with only the briefest of nods from Regan, and even less from Gwayne.

CHAPTER EIGHT

GWAYNE hadn't been waking so early for the last few days—mainly because she seemed to have so much trouble getting to sleep in the evenings—and on the day of the gymkhana she was woken by Donna frantically shaking one exposed shoulder.

'Wake up, Gwayne, wake up! You're missing all the excitement!'

Blinking away the last traces of sleep, she obediently did as she was ordered and, propping herself up on her elbows, gave her friend a frowning look. 'What excitement?' she queried.

Donna made an expressive movement with her hands. 'Brad's gone!' she announced dramatically.

'Gone?' Gwayne shook her head uncomprehendingly. 'What do you mean, *gone?*'

'Just what I say, and just as you predicted! He's taken himself off without a word to anyone ... oh, except for a short note he left for his aunt,' Donna added negligently.

Gwayne brushed a bright cloud of hair behind her ears and tried to assimilate what she was being told. 'You mean, he's gone on a prospecting trip instead of going with us to the Halfords' as he finally agreed?' It had been an extremely grudging agreement, she recalled.

'No! That's not what I meant,' Donna exclaimed vehemently. 'He's taken all his gear, and the car, and gone back to Sydney. The miserable crook has left us all stranded!'

'Oh, you must be mistaken, surely!'

'You think so?' Donna's expression was highly sceptical.

'But why?' Gwayne asked in bewilderment. 'We were due to leave the day after tomorrow anyway.'

'Who knows?' The other girl flopped down on to the side of the bed and grinned sourly. 'Although I can make a pretty good guess.'

Gwayne sent her an intent look. 'Like what?' she queried.

'Well ...' Donna began impressively. 'As you might imagine, quite a few strong words have been spoken so far this morning by one person or another, and along with those words some very interesting pieces of information have come to light,' was relayed with a flourish. 'It seems there was some sort of affair held here on Fairfax Downs the last time Brad deigned to visit his relatives, and dear Bradley not only hit the bottle so hard he was well and truly plastered by lunchtime—which I gather didn't exactly make him anyone's favourite—but he also began ranting and raving about how he should have been the rightful owner of the station and that Regan's mother—don't ask me how—had done him out of it all!' Her mouth turned down wryly. 'Taking a quick guess, I would say that's why he's done his little moonlight flit. Even *he* would be too embarrassed to face all Regan's neighbours again after a performance like that!'

'He still didn't have to take it to extremes by going back to Sydney,' Gwayne retorted.

'Mmm, well, I suspect that may have been his way of exacting revenge.'

'Because I refused to accept his preposterous ultimatum?'

Donna nodded. 'And because Warren and I sided with you over it!'

'Oh, hell, if it wasn't for the fact that we've been left out on a limb, I'd say good riddance to him!' Gwayne burst out, anger beginning to take the place of astonishment. She glanced ruefully at the dark-haired girl who was now lying diagonally across the bed on her stomach, her chin resting on steepled hands. 'I don't suppose Warren's come up with a way for getting the three of *us* back to Sydney, has he?'

'Uh-huh!' Donna flicked at a long strand of hair unconcernedly, then suddenly grinned. 'But Regan has. It appears I will be getting to ride in that gorgeous little flying machine of his after all.'

Gwayne's amazement certainly wasn't feigned. 'You mean, he's offered to *fly* us all the way back?' she gasped.

'Well, he's certainly not intending to drive it down the highway,' drily.

'But we can't let him!' Gwayne protested. 'It's not his fault we've been dumped on his doorstep.'

'Oh, stop worrying,' recommended Donna placidly. 'He says he expected to have to go down on business within a day or so anyway. Besides, if he doesn't take us, how are we going to get home? I don't know about you, but I doubt I've got enough to cover my fare by bus, plane, or train ... and I definitely don't cotton to the idea of thumbing a lift.'

'No, I suppose you're right,' came the reluctant acceptance. Then jerkily, 'How—how did Regan and his aunt take the news? Were they very upset?'

'I think Miss Fairfax was a little, but as for Regan ... well, I don't think that word's quite strong enough to cover his reaction,' Donna grinned as her eyes widened significantly. 'Just remind me never to get that man mad at *me*, won't you? I reckon if he could have got his hands on his cousin he would have half killed him! As it is Brad certainly won't get away with it scot free. This has even aroused Warren's easygoing nature, and when both he and Regan go calling on him the day after tomorrow ...' She allowed her statement to trail away with implicit meaning, before adding a slightly malicious, 'I have the feeling that young man will probably end up thoroughly regretting this impulsive action of his.'

More than likely, Gwayne meditated ruefully, but that didn't really make her feel any better. She didn't want to be beholden to Regan for providing their transport home, and especially since she couldn't help feeling at least partly responsible for Brad's abrupt desertion. Maybe if she hadn't told him about Simon until the matter was finally solved—as had been her original intention—then their holiday might have ended on a far less spectacular note.

'Now don't tell me you're feeling sorry for him,' Donna's voice broke in amusedly on her thoughts. 'You've got that look on your face I know of old.'

'Well, I can't help wondering if I shouldn't have ...' Gwayne began hesitantly, only to have her friend interrupt with an admonishing,

'Forget it! From what I can make out Brad's been building up these resentments of his against Regan from long before he met you, so I doubt there was anything you, or anyone else for that matter, could have done to stop him,' as she pushed herself up into a kneeling position. 'In any event, there's not much we can do about it now, so how about you getting a move on, then we can get over to the Halfords' nice and early and before it gets too hot,' she suggested with an expressive twinkle.

Gwayne's eyes lifted to hers wryly. 'I didn't think we had a vehicle now.'

'No problem,' Donna waved such a drawback aside carelessly. 'Regan's said we can use one of the four-wheel-drives.'

Another case of their having to presume upon Regan's hospitality? Gwayne mused, dissatisfied. And Miss Fairfax; how did she view being saddled with her nephew's friends? Donna had said she was upset at Brad's departure, which wasn't surprising, but their continued presence was hardly likely to make her overjoyed either, was it? A very unsatisfactory situation all round, but unfortunately not one she was in a position to do anything about, she realised glumly.

In actual fact a large percentage of Charlotte Fairfax's dismay at her nephew's conduct was on *her* behalf, Gwayne discovered to her astonishment when, on meeting the older woman in the dining room for breakfast, she had attempted to apologise not only for Brad but for the inconvenience his action had caused.

Charlotte had immediately countered that Brad's feelings had, unfortunately, never been a secret to them and that, although she found his latest inconsideration very disappointing, her greatest worry had been that Gwayne would have suffered a deep shock and hurt because of his thoughtless and self-indulgent defection.

As Regan had also been present at the table it had been somewhat difficult to convince his aunt that although she might have been shocked, it definitely hadn't caused her any emotional distress—not of the type Charlotte Fairfax was imagining anyhow!—without actually revealing just how little she cared now whether Brad was with her or not. Involuntarily, she had glanced at Regan when her deliberately misleading speech was finished, but had been unable to tell if her endeavours were successful or otherwise. Not by so much as a flicker of an eyelid had he disclosed what he was thinking, and finally Gwayne had had no choice but to turn back to her meal with a stifled sigh, and trust that luck was on her side.

'Well, we made it,' Warren grinned, not without some relief, a few hours later as he followed Regan's dark green Premier into the already filling area which had been set aside for parking at Copeland.

It had been a relatively fast journey, but not an entirely easy or comfortable one, for unless one knew the road well, there was a myriad of potholes and deceptive ruts to punish a vehicle and its occupants. Warren, it seemed, had managed to discover most of them!

'But not in one piece, worse luck!' teased Donna as she and Gwayne put their feet to the ground and began to flex aching muscles experimentally. 'You sure did your best to make it a trip to remember.'

'That's gratitude for you,' he winked at Gwayne. 'We'll let her drive us home and then we'll see how well she goes, eh?'

Gwayne shook her head vigorously—she knew as well as Warren did what Donna was like behind the wheel —and chuckled, 'No, thanks! It wasn't so bad that it's aroused suicidal tendencies.'

'Friend!' Donna pulled a laughing grimace at her. 'You just wait until the next time you want to borrow my new record player.'

Seeing that Regan and his aunt, as well as Nora and Stan Wallace who had journeyed across with them, were already engaged in exchanging greetings and conversation with friends, the three of them immediately began heading past the stalls which had been erected and were selling an amazing variety of wares to where a large proportion of the crowd had gathered to cheer on the participants in the specially constructed steer riding arena. As all the vantage points around the ring had already been taken they made use of one of the many small stands which were available to give them a better view of the proceedings.

It was dusty, noisy, and hot, but it was also exciting, and Gwayne watched each of the riders as they were bucked, spun, and jolted around the enclosure with her breath catching in her throat. How any of them managed to cling so tenaciously to those plunging beasts for as long as they did she would never know, but amid that friendly jostling crowd beneath a wondrously clear blue sky it was a spectacle guaranteed to enthrall.

They cheered loudly, as did many others surrounding them, when Les the stockman from Fairfax Downs stayed seated—if it could be termed that—for the allotted time, but when Donna and Warren suggested their throats were advising that they patronise one of the drink stalls Gwayne elected to stay and watch a few more rides before joining them.

A moment later she noticed a group of three leaving the rails around the arena—by their conversation as they passed Gwayne's stand they were clearly of the same mind as her friends had been—and intending to take their place, she jumped lightly down to the ground and took a step forward. Before she was aware of what was happening a savage grip had been placed on her arm and she was swung behind a large tree at the back of the stand by an evidently enraged Arleen.

'I didn't think you would have the nerve to come here today! Not to *my* home of all places!' the blonde girl hissed.

Rubbing mechanically at the scarlet marks left on her arm, Gwayne felt her indignation soaring. 'And if I'd known this was the sort of treatment you normally hand out to visitors I probably wouldn't have come,' she retorted. 'Just in case no one's told you, your manners leave a lot to be desired, Arleen!'

'You expect courtesy?' came the scoffing sneer. 'After what you're trying to do?'

What on earth was she talking about? Gwayne's brows lifted ironically. 'All I'm trying to do is get a closer look at the steer rides. If that's not permissible, surely you could have devised a less theatrical way of telling me.'

Icy blue eyes stabbed at her cruelly. 'I wouldn't try passing it off as a joke if I were you. Believe me, no one else round here thinks it's at all funny.'

'Look ... !' Gwayne's patience was rapidly running out. 'If you've got something to say, then for heaven's sake say it, so I can go back to watching something more pleasant. As far as I can see this—er—conversation is a complete waste of time. I haven't a clue what you're going on about!'

'And how you'd love me to believe that, wouldn't you?' The sneer was back again in full force. 'Well, just so you don't continue to think you can get away with playing dumb, I'll tell you, but you'd better hear me good if you know what's best for you!' Arleen threatened spitefully. 'You and that gutless wonder Regan is forced to call his cousin—where is he, by the way, drinking himself into a stupor as usual?—well, the pair of you haven't been quite so smart as you think you have. You didn't honestly expect we would stand by and let you pass yourself off as my uncle's daughter, did you?'

Those last words had Gwayne's eyes widening as

comprehension dawned. 'Simon Houghton's *your* uncle?' she gasped.

'That's right!' For a moment the older woman looked smug. Then her expression reverted to one of cold malevolence. 'And I'll see you in hell before I let a nameless little nothing from nowhere rob me of *my* inheritance!'

Uncle? Inheritance? The revelations were coming too fast for Gwayne to absorb them and her forehead creased with a frown.

'Yes, I thought that would wipe the smile off your insolent face,' Arleen smirked pleasurably. 'It's not such a prosperous proposition now that you know someone else has a prior claim to Murramai, is it?'

'There never was any proposition,' Gwayne countered swiftly, feeling Arleen had had it all her own way for too long. 'I met Simon purely by accident and the suggestion that I might be his daughter came from him ... not me!'

'Oh, sure! Only that's not the way I heard it,' Arleen jeered. 'So why don't you and your unwelcome boyfriend do us all a favour and leave, hmm? Before we're compelled to suffer the humiliating scene of seeing Simon denounce you publicly as nothing but a golddigging fake!'

Now that just didn't ring true! 'I still think I'll wait and hear what he has to say all the same,' Gwayne's warm sherry-coloured eyes sparkled defiantly.

'Not if I have anything to do with it, you won't!' Arleen almost shouted in her irritation. 'You stupid little bitch, can't you understand I'm trying to save you some embarrassment? I know how the people round here feel about you. You're *not wanted*!'

A tall figure abruptly emerged from the other side of the tree to lean one shoulder against the broad trunk, fingers hooking indolently into the wide belt accentuating a lithe waist.

'Jumping the gun again, Arleen? You're doing that quite a lot these days,' Regan drawled. But clearly his words carried a greater significance for the tall blonde than they did for Gwayne, because Arleen's face went scarlet. 'And as for talking about saving embarrassment,' he continued softly, 'might I suggest you lower your voice a degree or two? You've had quite an interested audience listening to your abusive tirade, and somehow I gained the feeling their sympathies were not for you.'

'I couldn't care that,' Arleen snapped her fingers contemptuously in the air, 'for their sympathies! I don't need any of them ... and least of all you!' she spat out bitterly before turning on her heel and storming away.

Confusingly, Regan appeared neither surprised nor perturbed by her parting shot, one eyebrow merely flicking upwards lightly and his mouth curving mockingly as he queried,

'Simon hasn't arrived, then, I take it?'

Gwayne ran the palms of her hands down the sides of her lilac-coloured slacks and gave an indecisive shrug. 'I wouldn't know, he may have. In any event, I'm hardly likely to be the first one to know, am I?'

'Aren't you?' he returned lazily. 'Contrary to what Arleen so confidently had to say, I think he'll be wanting to see you very much.'

'Maybe.' She didn't intend to commit herself too far. 'We'll just have to wait and see, won't we?'

'Uh-huh! And in the meantime ...' Suddenly every vestige of indolence vanished as he swooped forward to enfold her wrist within his long fingers and she found herself being towed unceremoniously along in his wake.

'There are a number of things I want to discuss with you.'

Surprise kept Gwayne acquiescent for the initial few yards and then anger raced to the fore. She was getting heartily sick of people thinking they could drag her around at will this morning!

'Let go of me!' she muttered resentfully through clenched teeth. It was bad enough being forced to go with him without making her objections so loudly that everyone else realised she wasn't going of her own accord. 'I don't want to go this way,' as they passed another drink stall and the large striped food marquee, 'I want to go back and see the steer rides!'

Regan's fluid steps didn't falter in the slightest. 'All in good time,' he smiled aggravatingly over his shoulder and, in a moment of absolute exasperation, Gwayne deliberately caught up to him and surreptitiously—but as forcefully as possible under the circumstances—hit him in the side as she seethed, '*I* mean *now*!'

For all the good it achieved she might as well have saved herself the bother, Gwayne reflected dourly. A fly could have done better, and would have been granted at least *some* reaction, she was sure! However, on seeing John Foster approaching she decided that perhaps help was closer to hand than she had believed and put on her widest smile to greet him.

'Can't stop, I'm sorry, John, we're just on our way up to the house. See you shortly. Okay?'

Gwayne swivelled her head round as they passed the doctor without stopping, her bright smile weakening to a faintly apologetic one as John grinned tolerantly and raised a hand in response to Regan's lightly spoken evasion.

'That was rude!' she censured wrathfully. 'You could have offended him.'

'I doubt it. John's not that thin-skinned.'

'Would it have made any difference if he was?' she demanded caustically. 'You obviously don't care that *I* happen to object to being hauled along willy-nilly like some great overgrown dog on the end of a lead!'

At the bottom of the steps leading on to the verandah of the impressive homestead Regan stopped briefly, his smoky grey eyes running over her appreciatively. 'Some dog,' he commented dryly.

A rosy flush crept over Gwayne's cheeks, but she refused to allow him to disconcert her altogether and fired back threateningly, 'And just to prove it, I'll damn well bite if you don't let me go! I don't know what it is with people like you and your girl-friend that you consider you can do as you please with lesser mortals, but *I—have—had—enough*! I only wish to heaven Brad had asked me if I wanted to go with him when he left!'

If anything Regan's grip tightened as, without saying a word, he determinedly jerked her up the steps and along the verandah. Turning the corner, he headed for a doorway at the far end, totally ignoring Gwayne's renewed and voluble protests. Behind them the door was slammed shut and there was only time for her to register that it was a sunroom—the outside walls consisting of full-length bamboo-curtained glass, the furnishings comprising luxuriously covered cane loungers and chairs—before she was swept inexorably into Regan's arms and his lips were parting hers with masterful proficiency.

Immediately her hands came up in an attempt to thrust herself free, but it was a futile battle when her mouth was already yielding willingly beneath his and her body was traitorously moulding itself to his rugged form. Without raising his head from hers Regan swung her lightly into his arms and crossed to one of the loungers, sinking down on to it with her cradled firmly against his hard chest.

Gwayne felt as if she couldn't breathe, as if she was drowning; sinking further and further into a sea of delight as his fingers untied the drawstring of her loose-fitting muslin blouse and slipped it from her smooth shoulders so his lips could wander unhindered over her sweetly perfumed skin.

In a daze her hands slid beneath the cool silk of his shirt to trail wonderingly across the warm bronzed skin of his muscular back, and knew in that moment by the involuntary movement of those rippling contours that she had the power to arouse him the same as he did her. A stirring thought she had no time to dwell upon when a burning line of kisses ended in the softly smooth valley between her rounded breasts and an inescapable hand captured her chin.

Darkened grey eyes locked with drowsy brown ones. 'Now tell me you would rather have left with Brad,' she was commanded huskily.

It just wasn't possible and he knew it! Not while her fingers still rested against his firm flesh and she could remember so vividly her response to the exciting touch of his lips and hands.

'I'm still waiting,' he prompted.

With a despairing shiver Gwayne shook her head, murmuring, 'You know I can't,' in a throaty whisper.

Releasing his hold, Regan traced the path of an unbearably sensitive nerve down the side of her neck to the throbbing base of her throat with a gentle forefinger. 'So where do we go from here, hmm?'

'I—I ... oh, please!' she pleaded brokenly as she

tried desperately to regain some sort of control over her rampant emotions. 'No matter what impression I may have given you, I'm—I'm not really not interested in having any—any short-term affairs.'

Regan determinedly lifted her from his lap and on to the lounger beside him. 'Only in wedding bells, orange blossom, and marriage certificates, is that it?'

And only with you, her heart cried achingly, as she promptly fled to the other side of the room to stand with her back to him so he couldn't see the tears that were beginning to squeeze under her eyelids. Only with you, she repeated, while her fingers shakily fastened her bra and re-tied the drawstring of her blouse.

'You'd better be!'

The lazy drawl was so close beside her right ear that Gwayne spun round in surprise, tears still evident on her thick lashes, even white teeth catching at a soft underlip.

'I'd better be what?' she puzzled nervously.

'Interested in marriage,' he elucidated softly as he reached out to draw her unresistingly close. 'You see, I'm not interested in any short-term affairs either.' A finger beneath her chin tipped her head backwards. 'I love you too much to be satisfied with that, sweetheart,' he groaned.

Gwayne swallowed convulsively, not quite certain she was hearing correctly. 'Are you asking me to—to marry you, Regan?' she breathed unsurely.

'If you'll have me.'

If she would have him? With a joyous cry she threw her arms around his neck and pulled his head down to hers. 'Just you try stopping me! Oh, Regan, I love you, I love you, *I love you*!' she interspersed each phrase with an ecstatic kiss pressed to his delightfully shaped mouth.

He eyed her mock-threateningly. 'And is that why you went to such pains to convince me you preferred Brad's company?'

'What else could I do?' She was able to smile light-heartedly about it now. 'It never occurred to me you would fall in love with someone like me. Someone without connections, without ...'

His lips were the most stimulating silencer she had ever known and it was a long time before either of them experienced the desire for words. Eventually it was Regan who broke away with a strangled exclamation.

'Hell! I can't take much more of this!' He shook his head unbelievingly. 'You're an almighty challenge to my self-control, sweetheart, and right at this moment you're on the verge of winning. I want you too much, I'm afraid.'

Gwayne leant back against strong securing arms, her face glowing. 'No more than I do you,' she confessed shyly.

In an effort to relieve the electrically charged atmosphere surrounding them Regan teased, 'I should think so too. Haven't I been trying to make you feel exactly that way from the first night I met you?'

'Have you?' Gwayne dimpled, delighted. 'Originally I thought you were only doing it to cause trouble between Brad and me.'

'Mmm, so you said that evening in the garden,' he recollected wryly. 'My God, it nearly killed me to leave you alone in your bedroom that night. By then you were well and truly under my skin and it took every ounce of restraint I possessed to walk away from you.' He cupped her face lovingly between his hands. 'Would you have let me stay if I had suggested it?'

'I don't honestly know,' she murmured truthfully. 'I knew how you were making me feel, but you were still

Regan Fairfax, wealthy grazier, etcetera, and I was still Gwayne Peters, obscure secretary, etcetera, and "never the twain shall meet" sort of thing. I—I didn't want to be just a convenient substitute for Arleen.'

His arms caught her proprietorially back against him. 'You certainly weren't that, my love,' he stated categorically, one hand smoothing over her rumpled curls. 'Besides, Arleen and I were never as friendly as you apparently believed.'

'And especially not today,' Gwayne twinkled irrepressibly as she remembered how the other girl had stalked away from them.

'Yes, well, I rather think she took exception to my bringing up something she would sooner have forgotten,' he drawled.

'Something about "jumping the gun"?' she quizzed curiously.

'Uh-huh! The last time I came over here she kept hinting what a profitable alliance it would be if I married her. I'm afraid I was somewhat blunt in my reply.'

No, he wasn't the type of man such a proposal would appeal to, Gwayne mused. He was too much of an individualist to deliberately further his holdings in that fashion, and too much of a male not to want to make his own running with a member of the opposite sex.

Her thoughts wandered on in the same meditative vein for a few seconds and then stopped abruptly. 'May I ask you something that's been puzzling me?' she glanced up with a slight frown.

'Whatever you like,' Regan grinned, but then went on to remind her, 'Although if I remember correctly, I made a similar offer once before and wound up by being told something to the effect that I was a spoilt rich snob. I'm not leaving myself open for another dose of the same, am I?'

'Of course not!' Gwayne laughed, reddening slightly at the memory. 'Not that it was altogether my fault, mind you, I'd only just met you then and first appearances can be deceptive. You couldn't have expected me to know you were actually a tantalising, tormenting devil, now could you?' she queried mischievously.

His lips curved into that slow teasing smile she had come to know so well and which had always set her senses aglow. 'Watch yourself, sweetheart, you're heading into dangerous territory,' he drawled. 'I think you'd better ask your questions before I start getting ideas as to a suitable punishment for that little remark!'

Tempted to find out what he had in mind, Gwayne thought better of it. It was hard for her to keep her feelings in check too.

'All right,' she smiled. 'What I've been wanting to ask is this. Why, if Brad's always so disagreeable when he's here, do you still invite him or allow him to come? I would have thought you would prefer not to see him at all.'

'And quite possibly that *will* be the case after this last episode.' His tone was cool and sharp, leaving Gwayne in no doubt that where Regan was concerned this time Brad had gone too far. 'Up until now, though ...' He shrugged and rubbed a hand ruefully around his neck. 'Well, I guess it's partly been due to regret that he feels the way he does, and partly out of respect for his mother. Not only is she my aunt, but I also have a lot of time for her. She's a very nice woman.'

'Yes, I know,' Gwayne nodded. Mrs Keogh had always been very pleasant to her. 'But has Brad always been so jealous?' she now asked.

'No, not always. The first time it was noticeable was just after my parents died. Perhaps that was when someone told him about his mother having known my father. I wouldn't know,' he shook his head lightly. 'It's a pity really, because when he forgets to feel sorry for himself he can be very good company, as I expect you know. He even has rare flashes of good humour every so often while he's *here*,' he laughed wryly.

'Mmm, I couldn't understand what was happening when we first arrived,' she recalled a little sadly. 'He'd never given us so much as a hint as to how he felt about you and Fairfax Downs when we were discussing the idea in Sydney. Then the longer we stayed, the worse he seemed to become.'

'Culminating in your news regarding Simon, I suppose?' he grinned.

Gwayne gave him back a glare of feigned fierceness. 'Oh, yes, that really did put a match to the powder barrel! I should never have listened to you, you know. He was most irate, and if I hadn't told him he probably wouldn't have left as he did,' she surmised unhesitatingly.

Regan, however, wasn't prepared to be so generous. 'That's pure conjecture if ever I've heard it,' he claimed in amusement. 'Brad's calling your holiday to a sudden halt was always on the cards ... he's done it so often before. This time he just gave it a new twist, that's all.'

'But if I had ...'

'Stop blaming yourself,' he commanded softly. 'Anyway, he's gone, there's nothing you can do about it, and I can't really say I'm sorry.' He bent his head to kiss her leisurely but extremely thoroughly. 'At least his departure gave me the answer to a problem I'd been wrestling with for some time,' he continued huskily some long intoxicating minutes later.

Gwayne sighed pleasurably. 'Oh, and what was that?'

'Whether you were, in fact, still interested in him or not,' Regan revealed drily. 'It wasn't until breakfast this morning that I knew for certain.'

'But how?' she looked up at him quickly and grinned. 'I thought I'd done rather a good cover-up job myself.'

'Fortunately, not good enough. That searching look you sent me when you'd finished was a dead giveaway, sweetheart,' he smiled so captivatingly that Gwayne was sure her legs had turned to water. 'If your charming little story had been true, there wouldn't have been any need for you to give me that look which asked, "Did he believe me?" as clearly as if you'd put it into words.'

'I'm glad I did, though,' she divulged throatily.

A confession which had him folding her even closer to his lithe form. 'So am I. It relieved me of a lot of worries because I had no thought of surrendering you to Brad without one hell of a fight, my love.'

'Oh, Regan,' she breathed tremulously. 'Whatever did I do to deserve you?'

To her surprise his mouth firmed and she could sense him keeping a tight rein on himself. 'You know, I really ought to tan your hide for that,' he reproved exasperatedly. 'You make it sound as if I'm doing you a favour when, in point of fact, you're giving me what I want most in this world ... yourself!' A hand gently brushed a stray lock of hair back from her creamy-skinned face and the action seemed to ease his tension. 'In the past you may not have had anyone to tell you how important you were or how much you meant to them, but I can assure you it's going to be very different in the future.'

'It already is,' she whispered dreamily as she leant

her head against his chest, a smile of sweet contentment curving her lips.

'Mmm, although there may be someone who doesn't agree I have the sole right in that regard,' he cautioned ruefully.

Brown eyes searched his wonderingly. 'Who?' she frowned.

'Simon.'

Considering recent events it wasn't surprising that he had been pushed to the back of her mind for a time, but now all those anxieties returned and she caught hold of Regan's arm nervously.

'Why? Have you heard something?' And before he could reply, 'Arleen implied that he hadn't been able to find the information he wanted.'

'I know what Arleen *implied*,' he countered significantly. 'But I also know that Simon would see you first before telling anyone else what he'd discovered ... no matter which way his enquiries went!'

Something Gwayne had suspected herself. 'Is he really her uncle?' she asked.

'Oh, I think there's some relationship there somewhere,' he relayed offhandedly. 'But as for it being that close, somehow I doubt it. Certainly neither of her parents are Simon's brother or sister.'

'She also said Murramai was her inheritance. If that is the case it could explain why she said what she did.'

'Sounds more like wishful thinking to me,' he laughed. 'It might be what Arleen has in mind, but I can't really see the same thought being in Simon's. As far as I'm aware, he doesn't even think that highly of her.' A delightfully satisfying kiss was pressed against her willing lips before he went on to suggest, 'Now, suppose we go and find out exactly what Simon does have to say, hmm?'

Gwayne nodded slowly, a trifle apprehensively, and with Regan's arm holding her reassuringly against his side they made their way out on to the verandah. At the top of the steps they stood for a time searching over the crowds which mingled below in a vivid scene alive with colour and movement. More visitors were arriving by the minute and it was difficult to distinguish one from so many.

'There he is!' Regan was at last able to pinpoint his whereabouts and indicated a group of three men as they stood talking outside the marquee. 'Shall we join them?'

Almost at the same moment Simon turned and, seeing them, murmured something quickly to his companions and began heading towards the homestead. The closer he came the more nervous Gwayne became and her hands clenched tightly at her sides.

'I can hardly stop from shaking,' she half laughed unsteadily as they walked down the steps.

He smiled down at her encouragingly, his arm clasping her tighter. 'Never mind, sweetheart, it won't be for much longer. Just don't be quite so hard on him, or yourself, this time, huh?'

'Oh, Regan, that was only because I was too scared to admit it might be true,' she explained shakily. 'Maybe I'm just stupidly superstitious, but I felt as if I would be tempting fate. If I agreed with what you were saying then it would have been proven wrong. If I didn't,' she hunched her shoulders helplessly, 'then maybe there was a chance.'

Only a few yards separated them from Simon now and Gwayne noticed an urgency in his step and a certain expression on his face which had her unconsciously holding her breath. He wouldn't have that look of restrained eagerness if it wasn't good news, would he?

As soon as they had exchanged rather strained greetings Simon whisked them away to some nearby garden chairs which had been arranged in the shade of a thickly spreading tree, one hand delving into his wallet and producing two old and somewhat tattered sheets of paper together with a crisply folded new one as he did so.

He could hardly wait for Gwayne to be seated before passing the two worn sheets into her nerveless hands. 'And just to be on the safe side, in case the thought crossed your mind, I've had them checked by an expert ... the handwriting's identical,' he smiled elatedly.

Amid a mounting tension Gwayne unfolded them swiftly, her eyes flashing cursorily over the contents of the first. It was apparently one of thse notes Simon had mentioned Judy Ashcroft having written to him from Sydney. The second, and her eyes rounded in astonishment when she saw it, was the note which had been left with her at the home. Even the pin marks at the top were still visible. Holding them next to each other for comparison, she knew there had been no need for Simon to resort to the services of an expert. The handwriting *was* identical, and so was the notepaper!

'So it is true—Judy Ashcroft was my mother,' she whispered shakenly, her gaze lifting incredulously to Simon's. 'But—but how did you get this?' as she indicated the second piece of paper.

'After many hours spent searching through dusty old records at the Children's Home with the unflagging help of a Mrs Coleman,' he informed her with an expressive smile. 'She was positive she'd kept it and I think she was almost as determined as I was to find it. That woman thinks a tremendous amount of you, little one.'

'As I do of her.' Gwayne spoke softly but with undeniable feeling. 'She was wonderful to all of us.'

Simon leant across and clasped one of her hands sympathetically, then flicked open the sheet he had kept until last and presented it to her with a flourish. 'Now to the *pièce de résistance*,' he announced with undisguised satisfaction. 'You've never seen that before, have you?'

No, she hadn't. Owing to the lack of information at her disposal it had been impossible for Gwayne to discover, but Simon happily had been able to approach the problem from a different direction and had uncovered the most incontrovertible evidence of all ... the registration of her birth! In black and white it answered every question she had ever wanted to know regarding her origins.

'Oh, Simon, I don't know what to say,' she cried helplessly as her fingers clutched at his and her eyes hastily sought Regan for support. 'I never expected anything quite so indisputable.'

'But you are pleased?' he probed anxiously.

She nodded vehemently, unable to put her feelings into words and tell him how much at that moment. 'Are you?'

'Unbelievably,' he laughed, but not without a slight crack in his own voice. 'I'm only sorry I had to spring it all on you so suddenly. It was just that I didn't arrive back from Sydney until yesterday afternoon and I wanted to tell you in person, not relay it over the radio with everyone listening in.'

Gwayne was thankful for his consideration. She much preferred it this way, even though she still felt a little overwhelmed.

Regan rose agilely to his feet and smiled at the older man in understanding. 'And now I guess you'd like some time alone together,' he surmised as his hand rested on Gwayne's shoulder tenderly.

'It would be appreciated—the more so since I suspect you've already stolen her from me,' Simon retorted dryly. He turned to Gwayne to question, 'Am I right?'

She nodded shyly while Regan smilingly offered an excusing but decidedly unrepentant, 'You have a very lovable daughter, Simon, who means a great deal to me. I wasn't taking any chances on losing her ... not even to her father.'

'Well, I couldn't wish to see her in better hands, and as Gwayne could have chosen someone who lives hundreds of miles away from here I won't complain—as long as you don't when I'm a constant visitor,' Simon chuckled.

'You've got yourself a deal!' Regan laughed in return, and bent to drop a lightly possessive kiss on Gwayne's forehead before leaving.

With her hand still clasped in Simon's, Gwayne watched his commanding figure stride away, her sherry-coloured eyes soft with adoration. She knew for a certainty that it wouldn't be long before he was back at her side. That was the way it would always be in future. Their future! But, in the meantime ...

She turned to the man beside her with a full heart. Four weeks ago she had been painfully alone in the world, but now ... now everything had been changed unbelievably! Not only did she have a father, but very shortly she would have a husband as well. In more ways than one had the Plains of Promise generously been true to their name this year!

Harlequin's
Collection
EDITIONS OF 1979

YESTERDAY'S LOVE
FOR ALL YOUR TOMORROWS

You relive your love in memories. Letters tied in blue ribbon...roses pressed between the pages of a book... keepsakes of a romance that will never be forgotten.

A great love story has a different kind of timelessness. It can be cherished in memory, but it can also come alive over and over again. Harlequin proved that three years ago, when we introduced the first 100 Collections—outstanding novels, chosen from two decades of beautiful love stories. Stories that are still treasured by the women who read them.

Now we are bringing you the Harlequin's Collection editions of 1979. Best-selling romantic novels that were written from the heart, giving them a brilliance that the passage of time cannot dim. Like a lovingly crafted family heirloom or a gift from someone you love, these stories will have a special personal significance. Because when you read them today, you'll relive love. A love that will last, for all your tomorrows.

$1.25 each

Choose from this list of classic Collection editions

Relive a great romance…
Harlequin's Collection 1979
Complete and mail this coupon today!

Harlequin Reader Service

In U.S.A.
MPO Box 707
Niagara Falls, N.Y. 14302

In Canada
649 Ontario St.
Stratford, Ontario, N5A 6W2

Please send me the following Harlequin's Collection novels. I am enclosing my check or money order for $1.25 for each novel ordered, plus 49¢ to cover postage and handling.

☐ 152	☐ 161	☐ 169
☐ 153	☐ 162	☐ 170
☐ 154	☐ 163	☐ 171
☐ 155	☐ 164	☐ 172
☐ 156	☐ 165	☐ 173
☐ 158	☐ 166	☐ 174
☐ 159	☐ 167	☐ 175
☐ 160	☐ 168	☐ 176

Number of novels checked @ $1.25 each = $ _____

N.Y. and N.J. residents add appropriate sales tax $ _____

Postage and handling $ _____.49

TOTAL $ _____

NAME _____
(Please Print)

ADDRESS _____

CITY _____

STATE/PROV. _____

ZIP/POSTAL CODE_____

Offer expires December 31, 1979

ROM 2283

And there's still *more* love in

Yes!

Six more spellbinding
romantic stories every month
by your favorite authors.
Elegant and sophisticated tales of
love and love's conflicts.

Let your imagination be swept away to
exotic places in search of adventure,
intrigue and romance. Get to
know the warm, true-to-life
characters. Share the special
kind of miracle that
love can be.

Don't miss out. Buy now and discover
the world of HARLEQUIN PRESENTS...